Last Minute Mermaid

Tallulah Burns

With thanks to

Bridget Essex
(for lighting the fire)

Gemma Dubaldo
(for guarding the flame)

And
Leisa Clark
(for accidentally coining the phrase
"Last Minute Mermaid")

Chapter One

To begin with, Lorelei Desciance lived in a mermaid cottage under the sea. Even though she didn't, really. It was complicated. Complicated and at the same time simple. She lived in a house called Undersea Cottage because her best friend, Troy Preston, was a real estate agent with an agenda. And Lorelei was a sucker. Troy - gorgeous, gay and glamorous - had been her friend and confidante for ten years, and she could never say no to him. He was sweet, manipulative and unreasonably charming. It was hardly fair.

In addition to real estate, Troy dabbled in theatre, ran his own catering company and wrote screenplays on a pristine vintage underwood typewriter because he was convinced that computers were only suitable for internet gossip sites, videos of cute baby goats and online dating apps which he read because they amused him. He had once catfished a prominent married local politician and then blackmailed him into voting for legislation supporting gay rights. A confirmed "elderly bachelor" at the ripe old age of thirty, he had lost the love of his life (a handsome brooding artist with dark eyes and a beautiful smile) to cancer two years earlier and had never stopped mourning him. When Lorelei teased him, gently, about getting back out into the world and meeting somebody, he would smile and flap his hand dismissively, softening the gesture by leaning over to kiss her on the cheek.

"Darling," he would say, "I have had true love already. No need to go searching for it when I already found it once. Lightning doesn't strike the same place twice. I have known true love and now I can die a happy man."

To this Lorelei would roll her eyes and poke him with a finger manicured in shades of blue-green and purple.

"You're going to die an *old* man," she would remind him, "and you're going to get plenty bored before that finally happens."

Despite her urging, teasing, prodding and hinting, Troy remained determinedly single, and kept a framed photograph of his Lost Love on top of the dresser in his bedroom, where a tiny candle always burned in a small frosted glass holder. He was not maudlin about it. He considered himself to have been blessed, and for that he was quietly grateful. Lorelei adored him. Falling easily into the role of wise best friend, he of course had no compunction about prodding her to find true love.

"After all darling," he would insist, over a glass of Pinot Grigio in the elegant dining room of his condominium. "*You* need to go searching for true love out there, because you haven't found it yet." He was convinced that out in the Great Wide World, there was an amazing, one-of-a-kind woman, just waiting for Lorelei to find her. As it turned out, he was right.

In the great grand scheme of mortifying predicaments (up to and including the legendary if apocryphal waking up in algebra class in your underwear) Kasey Martin would place her current position—posing fetchingly in the center of a massive and professionally embellished seafood buffet—in at least the top five. Possibly the top three. When Troy Preston, her closest and arguably dearest friend (they argued a lot) had called to beg her for help the night before, she had agreed out of habit and the kindness of her heart, and she was currently regretting both impulses.

Convinced by Troy to fill in at the last minute for a themed formal corporate banquet, she had presumed her contribution to the prevention of the ruination of Troy's struggling catering company would take the form of carrying chairs, placing floral arrangements, or – at the worst – serving champagne or bussing tables. By the time she discovered his plans included dressing her as a mermaid and placing her on the buffet table as a live centerpiece, it was far too late to bow out gracefully. In fact, it was far too late to do anything gracefully; the beautiful but weighty green lame' and sequin mermaid tail he had squeezed her into was held in place with Velcro and strategically hidden duct tape, and precluded anything requiring balance, movement, or athleticism. Like walking.

Needless to say, 'living centerpiece' was the last thing Kasey had expected when she became an actress, and she felt quite certain that her new and still fairly shiny theatre arts degree was at home hiding its head in shame, leaving an empty frame on the wall of her apartment. If it was not already at the greyhound station boarding an outbound bus in the equally mortified company of her voice lessons and her tap shoes. Suppressing an eye roll (if drama school had taught her anything, it was resting non-bitch face) Kasey sighed.

In light of recent events, she thought, she ought to probably be grateful to Troy for calling her at all – even for a favor – considering that since her latest breakup, her conversational skills had been more or less reduced to sniffling, hiccups and wine cooler flavored blubbering. For the past month, while Kasey's gorgeous and unrepentant ex-girlfriend (the beautiful Cassandra, goddess of infidelity) swanned around town on the arm of a high powered lawyer who wore Gucci power suits and Christian Louboutin stilettos, Kasey had hidden in her new, half unpacked apartment, wearing worn yoga pants and faded Broadway show T-shirts, determined to never again give her heart to a woman. Or a man. Unless the man was a beagle. Or a beverage. Or lived in a one pint carton. Other than Troy, her only companions for weeks had been Jack (Daniels), Ben (and Jerry) and the dog belonging to her neighbor. The dog, a black and tan bundle of wagging and whuffling, greeted her in the apartment parking lot every morning with more enthusiasm than Cassandra had ever greeted her, and Kasey appreciated the effort.

Cassandra. Pushing the thought from her mind, Kasey sighed again – this time in relief – glad that her ex-girlfriend would never know that she had subjected herself to the degradation of dressing as a mermaid at an "Atlantis" themed corporate party for the city's most prestigious law firm. Forcing a smile, she set her teeth as she held aloft a silver tray of scallops along with the shreds of her pride. At least she knew that Troy would never tell; he had always hated Cassandra.

Shaking her head to disperse the all too recent technicolor memories of breakups, cheating girlfriends and U-Haul trailers (she had vacated the luxury of Cassandra's condo within thirty minutes of finding out about the other woman) Kasey pasted on a desperate smile, and nodded with fond, exasperated malice at Troy, who waved enthusiastically from the other side of the enormous banquet hall, but stayed wisely out of range of Kasey and the tiny silver fish forks with which he had unwisely armed her. Troy was nothing if not well versed in self preservation.

Caught up in vivid and colorful daydreams of wreaking vengeance on her best friend for turning her into a glorified serving platter, Kasey froze suddenly, as the drone of voices around her seemed to part for a moment, and a clear voice cut through the muted clamor, a high, tinkling laugh – fake and familiar – echoing a clever comment and purring in the reaction of its admirers. Suddenly feeling her blood run cold (and wondering irrationally whether mermaids were technically warm or cold blooded creatures) Kasey closed her eyes in mortification, as a glamourous woman in a tailored Giorgio Armani tuxedo that showed off her expensively maintained figure stopped directly in front of her, one eyebrow raised and a mocking smile playing over her perfectly sculpted lips.

"My goodness, Miss Carat," the woman purred, smooth and sophisticated and clearly worth every penny of the exorbitant fees her law firm clients paid her. "Just look what is gracing the seafood table!"

Kasey felt the last of her pride shriveling on the vine. Carat. Cassandra's last name was Carat. Carat, not carrot, like the vegetable. Spelled carrot, the name might have been undignified, quirky, possibly even a little bit endearing. And vegetables, her mother had always insisted, were supposed to be good for you. But no. Cassandra was Carat. Carat, like the diamonds. Beautiful, yes, absolutely. But also cold and hard and expensive. Carat. A name unusual enough that it was almost a foregone conclusion that two women in a city the size of Bloomington Indiana probably would not share it. Which meant that . . .

Her skin prickling, her eyes burning with the real and very probable threat of tears of embarrassment, Kasey found she could not look away, and felt her face flooding scarlet as the woman's escort turned, champagne glass in hand, her surprise at finding her ex-girlfriend dressed as a mermaid swiftly replaced by a mocking smirk.

"You never could say no to Troy, could you?" Cassandra said with a shake of her perfectly coiffed blonde head. "Honestly, Kasey, have you no dignity at all?"

Chapter Two

The champagne fountain, aesthetically lit cascades of iridescent foaming bubbles tumbling from great heights to artistic effect, was probably not deep enough to drown in, but Kasey was hopeful that she might manage it. Trapped as she was on the buffet table, bound in place by mortification and mermaid accoutrements, she settled instead for the unlimited alcohol afforded by proximity and expensive crystal stemware.

The graceful reach of her arm – her movements enhanced by years of dutiful dance classes – tipped the delicate flute into the champagne every time Cassandra's clear laugh rang out across the ballroom, or a flash of her expertly arranged hair caught the light. After giggling insultingly into her drink and slipping her arm through the arm of the designer lawyer she was apparently dating, she had not given Kasey a second glance, which was a mercy.

Vaguely aware of the bubbles going to her head, Kasey slowed her determined consumption, supposing wryly that with Troy's expensive and elegant taste, she probably should not be draining the champagne fountain like she was getting free refills at McDonald's. Then again, maybe she ought to – Troy owed her.

Turning deliberately away from the image of her ex-girlfriend swirling and spinning in the arms of a tuxedoed barracuda, Kasey sent her gaze in the other direction, noticing for the first time that another buffet table graced the other end of the banquet hall, just beneath a glittering chandelier and set at right angles to her own. Catching her breath, she set her champagne flute down without looking, scarcely noticing when it tipped, its contents scattering across the fabric of the mermaid tail like iridescent jewels and sea water. On the other table, was another mermaid.

Of course, the appellation did not do the reality justice. "Another mermaid" implied that some other unwary actress, swept away by Troy's innocent smile and deceptively dangerous charm, huddled miserably between elegantly arranged towering edifices of shrimp and clams and mussels, and avant garde ice sculptures meant to represent – as near as Kasey could tell – either Jason Momoa or Poseidon (Troy's tastes were eclectic). This mermaid, the *other* mermaid, did nothing of the kind.

Turning to glance over one shoulder, the woman on the opposite buffet table instead laughed suddenly at something Troy had said, twirling a silver serving fork between nimble, elegant fingers and showing no inclination toward stabbing him with it. She did not appear embarrassed to be wearing a tail, to be reclining among gourmet seafood sampler platters, or to be poised – hemmed in by appetizers – like a living, breathing piece of sculpture. In fact, she seemed to be enjoying it. Kasey realized she was staring but kept doing it anyway.

Resplendent in a blue and green mermaid tail and bikini top, the other mermaid laughed and chatted, smiled and dazzled, tossing turquoise dyed hair over her shoulder as she mixed and mingled without leaving her table, never for a moment acknowledging the ridiculousness of the situation or the part she was playing in what should have been an embarrassing display. What looked like a dozen bracelets, all glass beads in ocean colors, encircled her slender wrists, glittery ribbons twined in her hair (which was cut in a bob so adorable Kasey considered making a salon appointment the very next day to copy it) and around her neck, strung on a slender string of costume store pearls, was a mixed media collaged pendant that said "*Mermaid hair, don't care.*" For a moment, the illusion was so real, the vision so beautiful, that the words 'enchantment under the sea' suddenly didn't sound like a cliché. Kasey found she was holding her breath and decided she should probably stop doing that.

"Lorelei," Troy's voice was cheerful and familiar, cutting through the blur of lights and champagne as he reached to help the woman down from the table. "You want to take home some leftovers?"

Startled, Kasey realized that the great banquet hall was nearly empty. Florescent lighting now replaced the blues and greens of the theatre lights Troy had rented, the musicians were getting their parking stubs validated and packing up their instruments, and the ice sculptures were dripping steadily into widening puddles of water in the gilded trays beneath them. Jason Momoa now looked like a Picasso rendering of Jerry Garcia, which was a crying shame, Kasey thought, nearly tearing up and realizing she was tipsy. At least Cassandra was gone.

Putting down the platter of leftover scallops, she set them aside for later, fully intending to demand a well filled doggie bag. Troy owed her for this entire embarrassing fiasco, her arm and shoulder were aching, and wait… had Troy called the other mermaid Lorelei? Seriously? *Lorelei?* Lorelei like the siren of the ocean? Lorelei whose beauty could lead sailors to their deaths out at sea? Lorelei of the legend, the fairy tale, the archaic German folk song? Shaking her head, Kasey started making her way toward the edge of the table by way of an undignified butt wiggle. Well of course the other mermaid's name was Lorelei, she thought glumly, heaving herself athletically over the edge and landing with both fins on the carpet. She was perfectly enchanting.

Teetering dangerously but determined to go home and drown her sorrows (was that a mermaid joke?) in a carton of Phish food ice cream (definitely a mermaid joke), Kasey turned her thoughts away from the enchanting Lorelei, and shuffled precariously, hobbled and tired, in the direction of Troy and the check that had better be in the pocket of that snazzy suit he was wearing. It had been a long night. Just as she reached them, captivated despite herself by the bright blue hair and vivacious features of the woman she continued to think of as "the other mermaid", Kasey tripped over her own tail, twisted her ankle, and landed face first on the carpet.

Chapter Three

As Kasey made her slow and mincing way toward the second buffet table, Troy was once again reenacting the same old song and dance, adding new lyrics and fancy choreography when Lorelei wouldn't listen. He was more than determined that she – one of his oldest and dearest friends – should not go through life alone. There were plenty of fish in the sea, he argued, one bad fish did not ruin the whole ocean, and Lorelei wouldn't find what she was looking for unless she took the plunge. Eventually he ran out of cheesy ocean metaphors.

Lorelei wasn't buying it.

"It isn't as easy as you think it is!" she protested. "I mean, women aren't exactly falling at my feet, Troy."

At that moment, precipitous and flailing, Kasey Martin tumbled head over tail (literally), and landed in front of her on the carpet. Troy did not miss a beat.

"Aren't they, though?"

Lorelei ignored him and hurried to reach a hand out to Kasey. "Oh my god, are you okay?"

Staring up from her ignoble position sprawled next to Troy's impeccable Prada spazzolato wingtips, Kasey was not surprised to find that Lorelei was even more beautiful up close.

"Is it possible to die of embarrassment?" she asked wearily, raising a hand to the spot on her head that had collided with the carpet.

Taking an elbow apiece, Troy and Lorelei hauled her bodily upright and set her back on her fins.

Lorelei looked doubtful. "I don't think it is."

Kasey shook her sore head in resignation. "Then I will probably survive," she admitted glumly.

Helpfully, Troy nudged them closer together. "Darling," he said, his look of concern theatrical and nearly convincing. "You might have a concussion." He elbowed Lorelei forward. "You shouldn't spend the night alone."

Both women whirled on him in familiar exasperation. "Troy!"

Removing the mermaid tail did not improve Kasey's mood as much as she might have expected, but it certainly made driving easier. Stopping her battered but trusty Nissan at an all night Starbucks to negate the nefarious effects of free champagne refills, she eventually made her way back to her apartment in the company of whipped cream, caffeine and sprinkles, and enough leftover seafood to last a week, if seafood could last a week, which she doubted. Considering, she decided not to risk it.

Weary but now too caffeinated to sleep, she showered and wrapped herself in an old burgundy bathrobe, then sank down on the sofa among unemptied boxes and unhung paintings, all the trappings of her old life waiting in the wings for her new life to open the curtain and start the show. Opening a bottle of wine, she set a wine glass on the coffee table and filled it, vaguely hoping that this latest bruise to her pride would prove fatal.

Draining the glass, she noticed that washing her hair three times had failed to remove the glitter and resigned herself to sparkling in the sunlight like a teenage vampire for the next few days at least. Glumly she refilled the glass, musing that at least when she died in anonymity (of terminal boredom and no social life) the forensics team could follow the trail of stale glitter to the scene of her demise. They might even suspect it to be a murder – which would be the most exciting thing to happen in the apartment since she'd been living in it. Shaking her head, long dark hair tumbling over her shoulders in still damp waves, she admitted she was pining, and didn't care. It had been a very long month of hurt and anger and upheaval, and she deserved to mope for a little while at least. After that she would have to unpack the boxes.

A sudden burst of music echoed brightly, causing her to jump, the wine sloshing over the top of the glass to splash against the back of her hand. Quelling her racing heartbeat, she realized it was only the ringtone of her phone and rose to answer its summons. She did not hurry. It's probably only Troy, she thought, still peeved about the mermaid tail. Who else calls me, after all? Moments after leaving the embrace of the sofa, she realized suddenly that despite the dedicated application of two iced cinnamon Dolce Lattes, she was still a little tipsy, a diagnosis painfully confirmed when she careened into the coffee table, tipping the half full wine bottle over directly onto the phone, which abruptly stopped ringing. Perfect.

Resigned (being angry took too much energy) she picked up the phone (now dripping supermarket quality Zinfandel onto the carpet) and carried it to the kitchen. Rummaging in a cupboard, she found a bag of rice and filled a bowl, dropping the phone into the tumbled pale grains and feeling as though she ought to scrub up like a surgeon before attempting the procedure. Musing that she'd bought the rice to try a fancy recipe, she shrugged and poured the rest of the bag over the phone. After all, who was she going to cook a fancy recipe for? That glorious sea siren from the buffet table? Angelina Jolie? One was as likely as the other. After all, who dated last minute mermaids? Leaving the phone to the medical ministrations of the bowl of rice, she gave up on the day and went to bed.

Chapter Four

Undersea Cottage, so named because it had been designed by an artist/architect with ocean going sensibilities, was different, quirky, artistic and utterly unique, if you liked that sort of thing, which Lorelei did. She did not resent Troy for brow beating her into buying the property (a tiny lot sandwiched between a multi-story office building and a row of high end condo units) because in the year that she had lived there she had fallen in love with the cottage.

Themed as if part of an underwater kingdom, the rooms – though small – were resplendent in blues and greens and silvery greys, with sinuous sea plants and faintly luminescent tracery gracing the walls from floor to ceiling. Ethereal, delicate and barely there, the designs were scarcely visible until the light caught them from above, or from one side, revealing a flash of curving petals or slender stalks, or fragile stems so delicate and graceful it was easy to believe – for the space of a moment – that the room was actually underwater, part of some mysterious and beautiful landscape.

Where most modern buildings boasted rectangular, symmetrical doorways, the doorways in the cottage were a series of curves and arches, almost as if they were natural entries to passages through an underwater grotto. Window treatments reminiscent of subaqueous plant life, and countertops inset with pieces of coral added to the illusion, and in a whimsical addition which Lorelei embraced more often than not, a hidden speaker system caused soft, subtle ocean sounds to play quietly in every room of the house at the push of a button. It was artsy and bizarre, yes, unusual and unexpected, but placed altogether, utterly exquisite.

Smiling (she often simply sat in the center of the cottage and loved it fiercely) Lorelei tuned off the practical, functional lighting that filled her bedroom, and switched on her night time lighting; flickering (if battery powered) candle flames and softly glowing Himalayan salt lamps illuminated from inside. Curling into bed, she stretched in luxurious contentment, the soft silk of her pajama bottoms sliding against her skin as she reached toward her bedside table for the piece of paper Troy had shoved into her fingers as she left the banquet hall. Drawing it out from under a large conch shell that rested on the top of the nightstand, she stared at it thoughtfully. Quickly marked out in Troy's neat, faintly persnickety handwriting was the name *Kasey Martin*, and a local phone number underlined with deliberation. Lorelei smiled indulgently, then rolled deep green eyes in fond exasperation. Troy was adorable when he was matchmaking, but he was also a pain in the ass.

Curling into the blankets, she turned her head on the pillow, the bright blue strands of her hair tickling around her ears, the paper still trapped between her fingers. Pale and white against the green-blue ocean colors of her nail polish and pillow cases, the paper waited, silent, expectant, and filled with possibilities.

Lorelei was curious. Kasey Martin, the "other" mermaid, had been perfectly lovely, she thought drowsily, drawing the blanket up over her shoulder as the air conditioning kicked on with a soft whoosh of ocean sounds from the hidden speaker. It wasn't as though she had anything to lose by asking Kasey out. After all, the worst thing the woman would probably say was "no", and the effort would at least get Troy off their respective backs for a little while. At least until he bounced back and renewed his efforts. If she had learned anything about Troy in the years she had known him, it was that his interference was a renewable resource. Lorelei shook her head against the pillow. She had known Troy for far too long to think he would be put off by excuses, logic or irritated demands to mind his own business. He was a traditionalist, a stickler, an old school meddler unafraid to poke his artistically aristocratic nose in where it didn't belong and keep it there for as long as it took to make things happen. Lorelei knew from experience.

Once Troy got an idea in his head (like mermaid tails and undersea cottages) he was like a dog with a bone. Or, more applicably, like a starlet with a tiara or a diva with a spotlight. He was convinced that since he had once been happy, it was his job to make certain that those he cared about had the same opportunity, and it was hard to stay mad at someone who only wanted you to be happy. Troy loved his friends fiercely and would do anything they asked of him (except of course butt out) and momentary exasperation had a hard time holding its ground in the face of his friendship and absolute loyalty. Lorelei didn't lie to herself; she loved her interfering busybody friend with all her heart.

Opening her eyes in the dim light, she stared again at the slip of paper, chiding herself for the silly romanticism of falling asleep with it in her fingers. It was only a phone call. A possible date. An innocuous and no strings attached reaching out to the sweet, shy girl with the long, pretty hair who had, after all, practically fallen from the sky – or at least from the buffet table. She had been lovely, that little brown haired mermaid, small and curvy and trying to hide a vague, indefinable sadness that made Lorelei want to rescue her. Shaking her head, Lorelei smiled faintly. Some sea siren she was, wanting to rescue people instead of luring them to their doom. A backward sea siren. An anti-nymph, a reverse underwater enchantress driven not to destroy but to… laughing softly, Lorelei hid her face in the sheet even though there was no one there to witness her embarrassment.

"Enchantress, Lorelei, seriously?" she muttered, sitting up against the pillows and reaching for her cell phone. "Just call the woman already. Do it for Troy."

Chapter Five

Kasey woke up the next morning to the querulous arguing of her next door neighbors and the loud and delighted shrieking of their unsupervised children, who were running wild under her bedroom window while their parents argued. Annoyed, but sympathetic, Kasey buried her head underneath her pillow and tried to feel charitable. The man and woman in the apartment next to hers argued a lot, and none of the arguments – heard clearly through open windows and paper thin dividing walls – sounded new. It sounded, instead, as though the couple, married none too happily, had been having the same arguments for years. Or perhaps the same argument, only in different sizes and colors.

Sighing, Kasey added another pillow to her fortress and tried to drown them out. When she and Cassandra had broken up there had been no repetitive arguments, no lingering resentments, no long, drawn out decline of the relationship. There had been the discovery of unfamiliar lingerie left in the bedroom, scented with perfume neither Kasey nor Cassandra wore, a sultry and explicit note taped to the door for Cassandra (not Kasey) to find, a tearful demand for an explanation, and – as requested – an explanation equal parts unapologetic and painful. Cassandra had found someone else, and – in the parlance of lawyers – was no longer a participating stakeholder with a vested interest in Kasey. Didn't Kasey think it would be best to move out?

Unsurprisingly, Kasey did, hurriedly throwing things into boxes with such speed and fervor that several of Cassandra's possessions had inadvertently entered the depths of the U-Haul, and several of Kasey's possessions had been left behind. The destruction of the relationship had been instantaneous and final, over in a moment, and had come without any warning.

Kasey, ingenuous and innocent, had thought that Cassandra was just preoccupied with law school, busy working overtime at the law firm where she was an intern, spending her evenings at the university library preparing for the bar examination. Cassandra had told her what she wanted to hear and made certain she believed it, even though her words had held no shred of truth.

Cassandra would make a very successful lawyer, Kasey thought sourly, giving up on sleep and rising to close the window with a snap, reducing the argument from next door to a muted distraction. She herself was entirely unversed in manipulation and obfuscation, and she could hardly tell a lie to save her life. It was what had caused her one night – in a bout of melancholy and too much Merlot – to confess to Troy that she was afraid she was somehow to blame for the implosion of her relationship with Cassandra.

Pouring her another glass, he had scolded her soundly for thinking anything of the sort, selected a few choice names for Cassandra and aired them with venom, refused to apologize for his language and offered to marry her on the spot. He didn't mean the proposal, of course, and Kasey didn't take him up on it, but he meant the nasty names he called Cassandra with every ounce of his perfectly ironed, Italian silk tie wearing being. Bless his heart.

Repairing to the tiny bathroom that adjoined her bedroom, Kasey dragged a brush through her hair, staring glumly at the glitter that now coated the bristles of the hairbrush. "Last minute mermaid," she muttered at her reflection in the mirror, recognizing that for the past month she had had the blues so bad she ought to have become a torch singer. It was no wonder she had no one in her life - her persistent state of gloom was even getting on her own nerves. Maybe Troy was right – annoyingly, he usually was.

Wandering out of the miniscule bedroom and across the cramped living room, she glanced at the coffee table in search of her cell phone before belatedly recalling that it was residing on the butcher block in the kitchen, nestled in a bowl of rice no longer destined for Shellfish Etouffee. So much for the recipe of the month club. Reaching beneath a tumble of dry grains, she noticed that her manicure was as in need of a pick me up as she was. The other mermaid (Lorelei, she corrected herself wearily, resigned to admitting that she was thinking about her) had worn nail polish in several shades of blue and green, the glorious cacophony of color as like the ocean as it was possible to be and still be acetone soluble.

Drawing the phone from the bowl, she gingerly pressed the on button, nostrils flaring at the scent of dried wine and sticky residue. On the surface of the phone, grains of rice were stuck in random asymmetrical patterns, glued in place by fermented grape juice, as if some psychotic sleepwalking artist had gone on a drunken midnight binge with hot glue and a vintage Bedazzler.

"Yes," she admitted to herself, picking a few grains free with a neatly trimmed fingernail, "I am that psycho."

Relieved, she felt her shoulders relax as the light on the phone blipped into life, the screen flaring briefly before getting down to business. A new cell phone was not in her budget at the moment. Her financial standing as a freelance actress and artist did not account for unexpected moves out of the condos of unfaithful girlfriends. The move – first and last month's rent, security deposit and U-Haul (plus the expensive bottle of wine with which she had bribed Troy to co-sign her rental of actual furniture) - had pretty much decimated her savings. Her scheduled expenditures for the foreseeable future included little more than Cup O' Soup noodles and drawing pencils; if she wanted anything more expensive, she would have to bribe Troy for that too.

Shaking her head, she stood in the kitchen, staring unseeing at the screen of the cell phone, taking a moment just to appreciate Troy. He was nosy and bossy, stubborn and pushy, but in reality, despite these idiosyncrasies, he was the truly best of best friends. Though she had been disappointed by life, by love, by the chances she had taken and those that she hadn't, she had never been disappointed by Troy. He had never let her down.

Shaking her head to clear it (and making an optimistic mental note to recycle the rice into something fancy after all and share it with Troy) she stared at a notification icon in the corner of the phone screen, innocuous and anonymous, and reached out a tentative finger to activate it. Hoping the missed call was not another unemotional message from Cassandra (who no longer cared about Kasey but wanted her Keurig and margarita mix back) she raised the phone to her ear, adding the scent of dried wine and rice to the glitter that still streaked her hair. The voice mail was not at all what she expected.

"Kasey? Hi!" The voice on the recorded message was breezy and confident. "So, I know this is weird. It's weird, right? You don't even know me. But Troy gave me your number and I wanted to call and make sure you were okay, since you bumped your head, and see if maybe you would like to go get a drink or dinner or something sometime. Oh, and this is Lorelei. Okay, well, I hope you're all right. Talk to you soon? Bye."

Stunned, Kasey turned the phone to face her and stared at the screen, quite certain that her voice mail was playing a cruel and terrible trick on her. Had she really just gotten a phone call – *a phone call asking for a date* – from the beautiful sea siren herself? Honestly, of the two of them, she'd have expected Angelina Jolie to call first. Finding she had wandered blindly out into the living room, she sank down onto the sofa. Lorelei was so beautiful. So confident. So – so much everything Kasey thought she would never be. Shaking her head, she marveled at the phone call, embraced it, celebrated it, but at the same time set it down in the center of the coffee table with the cell phone, untouched, unanswered, unacknowledged by anyone but herself.

Receiving a phone call from the beautiful and mysterious Lorelei was after all a wonderful thing, but right along with it came the expectation that the call would be returned (intimidating!) and that the invitation would be accepted (oh god!) or declined (impossible!). Fresh from a whirlwind of betrayal and heartbreak (why had she ever believed in Cassandra? Kasey thought bitterly), the idea of dating again, even casually, was beyond uncomfortable. It was terrifying. Even more terrifying? The realization that – as indicated by the butterflies in her stomach and the flutter of her heartbeat – it would be all too easy to fall for Lorelei (what was her last name?) Lorelei-other-mermaid without even meaning to. And as Kasey knew all to well, it wasn't the fall that hurt in the end, it was always the landing.

Raising a suspicious eyebrow at the cell phone, which sat in the center of the coffee table in silence, she chewed the edge of a gently curving thumb nail, feeling the tightness in her chest cheerfully turning a mole hill into a certified mountain. Should she call Lorelei back despite her hesitation and reservations? Go for drinks? Break her vow to never date again? At the moment she was tempted to remain single, alone and miserable for the rest of her life on purpose just to spite Troy. This was all his fault.

Reasserting itself, reason stared at her with a reproachful expression. What was Troy's fault, exactly, other than the stupid mermaid tail? it demanded. A phone call from a gorgeous sea siren? An actual invitation to drinks or dinner? A better-than-Angelina-Jolie opportunity to get to know someone so amazing she made lying on a buffet table in a mermaid tail look like a god-given calling? Reason stared Kasey in the eye with a disgusted expression.

Snatching the cell phone from the coffee table with a martyred expression, Kasey swiped a finger across the screen, the wallpaper photo of she and Troy at the Lake Monroe beach smiling up at her without apology.

"Jerk," she whispered, making a face at him, but the name calling was fond and without any oomph behind it. On the phone screen, Troy smirked knowingly, and Kasey set the phone face down on the sofa and built a pillow fort around it. She wasn't enough for a woman like Lorelei, she thought desperately. Not smart enough, not worldly enough, not flashy enough. Sighing, she stared at the mound of pillows and admitted the truth. What she really was not, was brave enough. Fleeing the living room and the cell phone pillow fort, she locked herself in the bathroom.

Bundling her hair into a messy bun of glitter, rice and last night's wine spill, she stared into the mirror, taken by unexpected surprise by the face that stared back at her. Olive skin and deep brown eyes gazed from the mirror in faint reproach, loose strands of sleek brown hair twined artistically over a forehead furrowed in thought, and an air of tragic whimsy, eclectic and creative, reminded her that she was – despite her current predicament – actually deserving of love and joy and happiness. Sadly, this did not make the road toward those things any less intimidating, but it did remind her that she was worthy of the journey. Raising a hand, she slid slender fingers through the tumbled tresses of her hair, itching to draw a self portrait of the girl she had caught unaware in the mirror.

"Mermaid hair, don't care," she whispered softly. Nodding, she offered the mirror girl a smile, suddenly loving her soulful eyes, her hopeful features, her wild, tumbled hairstyle. She needed to love the girl in the mirror, she realized. After all, they were in this thing together.

Chapter Six

Fully aware that her picture was probably already printed in the dictionary under the section "hopeless coward", Kasey did not call Lorelei back, though for a short and delusional while she pretend that she was going to. The half unpacked apartment reaped the benefits of her denial driven procrastination, and was soon a three quarters unpacked apartment, with newly hung curtains, alphabetized refrigerator shelves and freshly vacuumed floors. Even the floors that didn't have a carpet. She stopped just shy of categorizing and filing the junk mail, recognizing that she was doing Zumba moves on the brink of stupidity. Eventually running out of excuses, she grabbed her current sketchbook and a zippered pouch of drawing pencils and left the apartment, not pausing to look the girl in the mirror in the eye as she fled. She knew was letting her down.

The pencil pouch, a glittery vinyl affair emblazoned with the command "Carpe Diem", would have narrowed its eyes at her if it had any, and she turned it face down on the seat of Nissan as she twisted the key in the ignition. She well knew that she was going to carpe the excuses instead and did not need a reminder. Grimly turning her attention to conscientious lane changes and meticulous turn signals that would have done a ninety year old Sunday driver grandmother proud, she headed into town.

Sunning himself on the private terrace of his elegant condo like a burnished jungle cat with a heat lamp, Troy Preston drew his high end cell phone out from under the latest copy of GQ magazine and thumbed the screen to life, angling his profile to its best effect in the sunlight. He was half convinced that the government was using infrared cameras and stealth imaging to spy on its most interesting citizens, and he felt he owed it to them to look fabulous.

Scrolling through the images in his phone gallery, he smiled as the screen paused on a picture of Kasey, taken secretly from across the room at the now infamous corporate banquet. Using an impressive telescoping ability gleaned from a pirated cell phone app, he had captured her with a tender, innocent expression, as if dreaming underwater, her hair curled gracefully around her features, her eyes gazing into the distance and her mermaid makeup rendering her enchanting and exquisite. Indulgently, Troy smiled. For some reason inexplicable to him (a man well acquainted with the gorgeous image in the beveled mirror that graced his bedroom wall) Kasey had no idea that she was absolutely stunning.

Smiling again, he activated another app that sent the lovely image in the direction of the wireless printer that rested in state on a polished nineteenth century credenza inside the condo. If Kasey needed proof that she was beautiful, wonderful, and worthy of love, he would give it to her. In a gilded frame. Smiling with the expression of a cat with a stolen bowl of cream, he activated the app a second time, deciding to buy a second gilded frame for when he gave the second copy of the lovely photo to Lorelei. The move was not subtle, but it was sophisticated and clever, and he knew it.

Master of gadgets and willing slave to the latest tech, Troy had a treasure trove of apps that could do almost anything, and he had cross connected every piece of electronics in his condo to operate in concert at the push of a button or the swipe of an icon. He was somewhat certain (and only mildly concerned) that he had once accidentally launched a space shuttle while operating the ceiling fan remote in his bedroom, but since NASA had yet to come and kick his door down with FBI officials and handcuffs, he was fairly certain that they had not known it was him. If, on the other hand, he was indeed under surreptitious government surveillance, he rested serenely in the security of knowing that hair looked unquestionably amazing.

Kasey, on the other hand, clearly lacked the inherited genetic ability of uninhibited self-promotion and needed a kick in the butt with a pair of size ten and a half imported Italian loafers. Which Troy just happened to be wearing. Having finally freed herself (if not by choice) from the emotionally damaging and manipulatively gaslighting clutches of Cassandra Carat, Kasey was going to have to come to grips with the fact that she was desirable, delightful and deserving of affection (which would be a de-licious de-bate, if he could only get her to talk about it.) Smiling with the air of a general marshalling his troops for battle (provided said troops were wearing Givenchy trim fit uniforms and professional quality hair gel) Troy cracked his knuckles, limbered up his thumbs, and started texting.

Chapter Seven

The local indie coffee house (called *Karma Sumatra)* had not been serving coffee when the University of Indiana first opened its doors in 1820, but it had long been the mainstay refuge of artists and musicians, students and theatre people in search of the eccentric, the quirky and the avant garde. The owner, Florence, ("Henderson, like the actress…but not," she was quick to point out) had opened the shop with little more than a vision, a working knowledge of wiring and drywall, and a source for locally produced artisan coffee and baked goods, and had become an icon in the Indiana town known for its artistic ways and diverse culture. A stubborn bastion of diversity and open minded thinking hemmed in on all sides by conservative republican objections, Bloomington had fought hard to be true to both its roots and its wings, and the coffee shop stood as a perfect example. Sandwiched between a Vintage clothing store, a new age crystal shop and a gay bar as quirky and eccentric as its colorful clientele, Karma Sumatra opened its doors early and closed them late, and in between welcomed all and sundry to the dim cool interior scented with coffee beans and creativity. Kasey loved it.

Standing for a moment at a long, graffitied wooden counter that had seen sit ins and write ins and grassroots revolutions, she turned her thoughts deliberately away from beautiful sea sirens and meddling best friends and breathed in the air of the place as if greeting a long lost family member. It had been far too long since she had been there. A wild and uninhibited explosion of oddball sensibilities and arbitrary eccentricities, Karma Sumatra blended such a cacophony of personalities that any psychiatrist worth his or her salt could make a lifetime career just out of cataloguing them. Kasey loved every cracked tile and lava lamp in the place.

Pausing to choose between a 'Three penny Java' (which cost five ninety five) and a seven dollar concoction called 'Ghost in the Caffeine', Kasey settled on a 'Spill the Beans' cappuccino (a median compromise at six fifty), and made her way down a twisting back corridor toward the brightly painted back room of the space. There, bright yellow walls adorned with images of Elvis, Nelson Mandela and the virgin of Guadalupe rose around her like a much missed and familiar embrace, and she sank into a chair at a faintly wobbly table, beside a turn of the last century fireplace whose locally quarried limestone bricks had been painted white. Between the edges of the bricks, penned in meticulous sharpie, were lines from Shakespeare, quotes by Gloria Steinem and bits of poetry by Robert Frost. On the mantel, which was painted electric olive green in defiance of the dictates of architectural digest and Martha Stewart, an antique delft porcelain five finger vase stood ready and waiting, bearing a bouquet of sharpie markers like a rainbow of ink and enticement, sharing the space with a bust of Salvador Dali that was wearing a vintage nineteen forties fedora. Setting her sketch pad and pencils on the black and white checkered Formica of a vintage table from a long defunct Bloomington ice cream parlor, Kasey let her eyes rove around the room, drinking in the glory of old vinyl records used as wall art, castoff recycled arm chairs and sofas, a vintage Wurlitzer juke box that only played Sinatra, Elvis and Bob Marley records, and a gutted 1950's Philco television repurposed as a fish tank. The whole chaotic, colorful place made her artist's heart happy.

Cassandra, she remembered vividly, had scorned not only the coffee shop but the street on which it resided, the beverages it crafted and the horse it rode in on. Grimly, Kasey shook her head and reached for her sketch pad. Cassandra be damned, she thought with a burst of injured loyalty. Like Troy, the coffee shop had never let her down, but Cassandra certainly had.

Curling her feet around the legs of the wooden chair (painted in exquisite and extravagant designs by a Pakistani art student from the nearby university) she nibbled on the end of her drawing pencil out of habit, staring at the blank page in front of her and waiting for it to tell her what it was going to be. As the ghost of an image began to rise from the paper, she slowly started sketching, unsurprised to find wide eyes, silky hair and a forthright, irresistible smile emerging from underneath her fingers. Turning the page on her preliminary sketches, she turned to a fresh sheet of drawing paper, transferring the idea and images onto the new sheet with careful movements. Reaching for her pencil case, she drew sage and blue and turquoise from the depths, delicate peach and rosebud pink, emerald green and ivory white, and began to bring the beautiful image to life.

Chapter Eight

Smiling inexplicably and humming a tune from an old Gilbert and Sullivan musical, Lorelei curled on the cushions of her sofa (green and blue and lavender confections chosen to go with the underwater walls of the living room) and drew her cell phone from the pocket of her jeans. Pretending to check the time, the weather, the headlines, she noted with a pang of disappointment that Kasey Martin had not called her back.

Restless, at the same time both happy and disappointed (happy she had met Kasey, disappointed that the meeting might be a one time experience) she drew a book at random from an overstuffed bookshelf and sat pretending to read it. In the silence, her watch – a bright pink, retro affair with mermaid tails for clock hands - ticked loudly, counting the seconds that passed (nearly seven) before she thought of Kasey again. Blowing a puff of air through her nose like an exasperated dolphin, she set the book down in her lap, knowing she was not fooling anyone, especially herself. She wanted Kasey to call back, wanted her to say yes to a date, wanted to know if her skin was a silky soft as it looked and if those deep brown eyes melted into molten chocolate when someone kissed her…

Shaking her head, Lorelei had the grace to laugh at herself. Molten chocolate? she thought. Seriously? What even, Lorelei, what even?

Sliding a wide green ribbon from her hair, she used the improvised headband to mark her place in the book, staring absently at the tracery of silvery sea plants on the living room wall, there and barely there at the same time. Like her common sense. It wasn't as if she had fallen for Kasey Martin, she protested silently, only to hear her own voice mocking her in disbelief from somewhere inside her head. She was…curious. She would readily admit that much. She was interested. Attracted. Hopeful. And she wanted Troy to stop texting her. Smiling suddenly, she wondered if Troy was bombarding Kasey with texts also. She was fairly certain he was. If there was one thing Troy loved, it was matchmaking – the more resistant the two parties were to the idea the better. Troy liked a challenge.

Rising suddenly, shaking her head in a flurry of turquoise silk, she reached for a green messenger bag she had left slung over the back of a chair, her fingers brushing against the mermaid scales airbrushed onto the surface. She had always been on board for the mermaid theme when it came to her clothes and hair and accessories. Lorelei rarely did anything halfway; in for a penny, in for a pound.

Nipping her car keys from a cobalt blue sea shell shaped bowl on a table by the doorway and leaving her cell phone on the sofa, she slipped out of the cottage and locked the door behind her. She really needed some coffee.

As always when she was drawing, Kasey soon forgot she was sitting in the coffee house at all, as the sun rose higher in the sky outside the windows and her cappuccino slowly cooled at her elbow. Sweeping across the paper in skilled and graceful motions, her pencils seemed almost effortlessly to capture the essence of Lorelei's vivacious beauty, and while she drew, time passed quietly without her hearing its footsteps. Glancing upward at last, nearly an hour later, she bit her lip in concentration, trying to capture the perfect curve of Lorelei's jaw, the arch of her confident eyebrows, the luminescent quality of her skin.

Studying the figure across the room from her, head bent over a book, she meticulously corrected her drawing, streamlining the graceful neck, narrowing the chin, adding strokes of shine and almost-mermaid magic to the glossy strands of the hair. Distracted, intent, focused only on her drawing, it took a moment for her to register that she was no longer drawing from memory, but from life.

On the other side of the back room, completely oblivious and immersed in her pages, Lorelei herself was curled up cozily on a faded green sofa, bare feet curled underneath her, and shoes discarded on the woven rag rug that served as a carpet. Her soft, pale blue jeans were worn and faded, a faint hint of skin showing at one ripped knee, and the peasant top she wore, blue and green with bright embroidered patterns, had slipped down off one shoulder, leaving a creamy expanse of skin to gleam in the overhead lights. For a moment, Kasey couldn't breathe.

The Kasey part of her, hurt and gun shy and attracted and conflicted, urged her to crawl under the table, leap to her feet, run from the room, pull the fire alarm—anything to avoid a face to face meeting with the exquisite woman who had called to ask her out (and why had she done that?) and not received an answer.

Heat and then cold flooding through her, Kasey swiftly averted her eyes to the floor, concentrating on the colorful patterns and forcibly slowing her breathing. She was being ridiculous, she knew. The floor, cracked old vintage tile set into concrete, had been coming apart for decades, and Florence – taking advantage of the sculpture and pottery classes of the university art department – had commissioned student artists to repair it. The students, creative bright lights with limited budgets, had created beautiful mosaics between the undamaged tiles, using marbles and sea glass and bits of broken vintage china to fill the gaps. It was wild and colorful, magnificently chaotic, and normally Kasey could stare at it for hours, but in that moment, all she could do was stare sightlessly downward.

Frozen in place, panicking for no good reason at all, she quaked as the artist part of her demanded that she stay, that she resume drawing, that she capture the shadows thrown across Lorelei's shoulder by the lava lamp on the window sill, the casual curve of her fingers around the binding of the book, the graceful feet that peeked out from beneath her, pale and sweet, with purple toenail polish bright and bold against the sexy blue curve of her...stop looking at her butt!

Her face flooding scarlet, her papers and pencils scattering, Kasey snatched up her art supplies and bolted for the back door that led into the kitchen, her artist self rolling its eyes in disgust as her coward self ran for cover. Elbowing past Florence, Jorge the pastry chef, and several startled baristas, she scuttled through the kitchen like a terrified crab, slipping out the back door into the alley and ducking behind a giant green dumpster.

Redolent with coffee grounds, rotting fruit and day old pastries, even the dumpster looked at her without pity. Ashamed to have acted so ridiculously, even if only in front of herself, Kasey buried her head in her pencil smudged fingers. "Is this really what you have sunk to?" she asked herself in disgust. "What are you, twelve?"

Startled by the sudden vibration of her cell phone, she jumped, her head colliding with a hard surface for the second time in two days. The bricks of the coffee shop wall looked apologetic, as tears started to her eyes, but Kasey knew they were tears of mortification. Pulling the phone from her pocket she found a series of messages from Troy.

Troy:
I know she called you.

Troy: Did you call her back?

Troy:
You should call her back.

Troy:
Are you ignoring me? I won't stop texting.

Troy:
Darling, CALL HER BACK!

Berating herself for being a coward unworthy of a date with a siren, Kasey gripped the phone in furious fingers, knowing that once Troy had an idea in his head he would be distracted by nothing less than a troupe of Chippendale dancers parading by in the altogether. Even then he would only be distracted for a moment. Sighing, she opened the touch pad. She knew she was not angry at Troy, but at herself. The truth (why was the truth always so difficult?) was that she wanted to go on a date with the lovely Lorelei. She just had to get out of her own stubborn way in order to do it. Troy clearly thought so too – the phone vibrated again.

Troy:
Just call her back.
You deserve to be happy.
I love you, darling.

Setting her jaw, Kasey nodded fiercely, taking the tender words to heart. She knew that Troy was right. She *did* deserve to be happy, to be loved, to be respected, damn it. Just because Cassandra had not done any of those things did not mean that Kasey did not deserve them. Raising a shaky finger and bringing up the call log, she hit return on Lorelei's number.

Chapter Nine

After all the angst and unnecessary drama leading up to the phone call, the end result was anti-climactic. Lorelei's voice mail recording was as bright and effervescent as she was, and Kasey forced herself to leave a fumbling message before she could second (or third or fifth or seventh) guess herself. Feeling a small but gratifying surge of redemption, she texted Troy and turned to gather up the belongings scattered around the spot where she had been sitting.

Kasey:

I did.

I do.

I love you too.

Reaching for the sketchbook she drew a page free from the center, wanting to look just once more at her drawing, to see if she had captured the essence of her subject, the unconscious beauty, the effortless confidence, the vibrant exuberance that was Lorelei. The drawing was not there.

Feeling the by now familiar heat and ice flooding her stomach, Kasey reached for the sketch book with horrified fingers, tearing it open and

searching frantically between its pages for the missing –
and suddenly incriminating - drawing. She did not find
it. With growing mortification, she realized it had to
have fallen out of the sketch book in the back room of
the coffee shop when she fled out the back door
through the kitchen. The room where Lorelei was
sitting.

Temporarily pleased with herself for having
returned Lorelei's phone call, Kasey now stared with
wide and desperate eyes at the back door of the coffee
house, reimagining every spy movie she had ever seen
as she contemplated how to sneak back inside and
retrieve the portrait before Lorelei could find it. The
fire alarm solution – though still illegal – suddenly
didn't seem nearly as unconscionable as before. The
situation was a qualified disaster.

Pulling herself together with difficulty (glumly
visualizing her picture in the dictionary migrating from
C for coward to S for stalker) she drew a deep breath,
slipped her pencils into her back pocket and slunk
toward the brightly painted back door.

Wriggling her bare toes in the flow of air current from
the wheezing old air conditioner wedged into the coffee
shop window, Lorelei smiled and sighed, feeling the
tension draining from her muscles as she stretched.
Raising her arms above her head, she felt her back
unkinking itself with a satisfying series of pops she

ruefully acknowledged she had to blame on the daredevil version of dance and gymnastics in which she had engaged as a teenager. In the ten years since her sixteenth birthday, she had learned to her surprise that she was no longer indestructible but had not yet begun to act as if she knew it.

Shaking her hair free from behind her ears, she rose from the comfortably sagging old sofa, forgetting for a moment the book she had set on her lap while stretching her legs. Frowning suddenly as the book tumbled to the floor, she recognized the reason for her distraction, and mentally gave it the name that belonged to it. "Kasey Martin," she whispered, bending to retrieve the fallen hardcover. "Who are you, Mermaid Girl?"

Hearing the faint swish of paper against ceramic tile, she watched with resignation as her art museum bookmark, a narrow strip of cardstock emblazoned with a reproduction of *A Mermaid* by John William Waterhouse, escaped the pages of the book and slid beneath the spindly legs of a table on the other side of the room. Sighing, she crossed the room and bent blindly to retrieve it, surprised to find her fingers brushing against a second piece of paper, concealed from view by the colorfully painted chair beneath which it had fallen. Pinching the sheet between thumb and forefinger, her errant bookmark forgotten, she drew out the sheet of drawing paper and stared at it, confused for a moment by the rush of recognition that filled her when she saw it.

The portrait some unknown artist had created was exquisite, vibrant, nearly living and breathing; a thing of celebration and joy and beauty, and clearly a labor of love. For a moment, Lorelei thought she was looking in a mirror. Turning the paper over and over in wondering fingers, she searched for an artist's signature, a clue of identity or hint of ownership, some explanation for how this exquisite rendering, perfect in every detail, had come to rest on the floor in a room that was empty except for Lorelei.

Glancing around at the vacant chairs and uninhabited tables, she shook her head in disbelief as the faint sounds of the open mic offerings from the other room sifted between chinks in the wall and drifted down the hallway. As she had thought, the room was empty, and she closed her eyes for a moment, trying to recall the faces of the people who had been there when she arrived earlier. Reluctantly, she admitted that she did not remember them, could not now picture them, had not even noticed them at the time, too caught up in thoughts of Kasey Martin to pay attention.

Catching her eye, a flash of color caught the light from above; a scatter of drawing pencils in blues and greens, resting just beneath the edge of an armchair, their sharpened ends pointing toward the rear door of the kitchen as if arrows indicating direction. Bemused, she bent to gather them, her fingers tingling as she held them, as if some essence of the artist who had used them still lingered on their surface. Shaking her head sharply, she dismissed the idea as ridiculous, even as she smiled at the thought of it.

Retrieving her bookmark, she turned to the blank side of the cardstock, using the blue-greeniest of the pencils to write the words "Thank You" on the back of it. Piling the pencils neatly on the green paint of the fireplace mantel, she propped the bookmark up against them, the Waterhouse Mermaid facing outward, as if beckoning the mysterious artist to make themselves known.

Smiling again, Lorelei stared at the portrait for a moment before tucking it under her arm and moving back toward the sofa. The image was not technically perfect, she thought, slipping her shoes back on and turning toward the hallway. The artist had done wonders with her image. Gone were the tired circles underneath her eyes, gone the freckles painted by the sun in recompense for daring to step outside without sunscreen as a natural strawberry blonde masquerading as a turquoise haired sea child. Gone, too, was the slump of her shoulders, her dance class posture abandoned in between shows and her body slouching happily against soft pillows and old sofa when exchanging stage persona for real life. Whoever the mystery artist was, he (or she) had looked across the room and seen only beauty.

Lorelei was surprised to realize that it did not bother her in the slightest that someone had been drawing her without her knowledge. For some inexplicable reason there was nothing creepy about the drawing, nothing threatening in the action, no sense of obsession in the portrait she held in her fingers—only appreciation and inspiration. There was such reverence in the strokes of the pencils, such care in the shading and shadows, such loving attention to detail: the picture was clearly a tribute. Cradling the portrait in gentle fingers, Lorelei left the coffee shop and set out for home, still smiling.

Chapter Ten

The back room of Karma Sumatra was empty when Kasey finally peered through the crack of the warped wood kitchen door, feeling doubly foolish for invading the kitchen space twice. A wild pantomime of tiptoeing and pseudo karate moves paired with surreptitious B movie inspired stealth tactics (executed badly) had taken her as far as the doorway, where she had crouched ignobly between a vintage brass plated cappuccino machine and an ancient copper samovar, trying to work up the courage to go out there and own her own fiasco. Amused glances and a knowing smile from Jorge, the resident pastry chef, completed the embarrassing scenario, which by now was missing only props and music. Kasey sighed.

A thorough search of the back room, hallway, and kitchen floor yielded nothing and Kasey soon resorted in desperation to searching the tiny restroom in the ridiculous hope that whoever had found the missing portrait (please let it not have been Lorelei!) had stopped to use the facilities on their way out the door, set the picture down and forgotten it.

The restroom, a half-steampunk cubicle hidden under the staircase, offered an avant garde art display including exposed pipes and an elevated toilet on a platform, surmounted by a massive mosaic of glass and plastic jewels. On one wall, a graffitied map of surrounding Bloomington was punctuated with foil stars and stickers, and an inverted pair of mannequin legs held extra rolls of toilet tissue between its plastic knees. On the opposite wall some ecologically conscious citizen had written "Less cars, more bicycles," in marker, under which someone else had written "Less bikes, more ponies!" Over both, some enterprising probable English major from the college had crossed out "less" and written "fewer." Of the missing portrait of Lorelei, there was no sign; even the mannequin legs professed to never have seen it. Lowering the toilet lid, Kasey sank down on the plastic and porcelain throne in despair, staring at the mosaic tile pattern of the floor. There had been the portrait, and there had been Lorelei, now both were gone. The (hopefully coincidental) juxtaposition of those two conditions did not bode well.

Realizing she was a grown woman sitting fully clothed on a public toilet and hiding from the world, Kasey reached for the bathroom key, which was affixed to a green plastic dinosaur from one of those plastic molding machines that used to populate tourist sites and amusement parks throughout the nineteen seventies. The dinosaur – a roaring T Rex with massive teeth and tiny little plastic arms – offered no suggestions.

"Some help you are," Kasey accused him, returning both key and dinosaur to the counter in the front room and exchanging a weak smile with Florence, who reached a calloused hand across the scarred wood to squeeze her fingers.

"Whatever it is, Sweetie," she said tenderly, "it'll all work out in the end. Things do, most of the time."

Nodding with an almost hopeful hesitance, Kasey waved a weary hand and slunk out through the front door, avoiding the sympathetic gaze of Jorge, who slipped a foil wrapped warm raspberry pastry into her bag as she passed him. As the door closed behind her, Troy started texting again.

Chapter Eleven

When Kasey returned to her apartment, feeling equal parts idiotic and embarrassed, there was a thick padded envelope pinned to her door, and for a surreal moment she thought that someone (Lorelei?) had returned her drawing, most likely stapled to a letter of protest and a swiftly obtained restraining order. A moment later, she recognized the handwriting on the envelope as belonging to Troy.

Not satisfied with unsolicited texting, Troy had clearly taken matchmaking matters into his own determined (and, Kasey suspected, subtly manicured) hands, and driven across town to the apartment to harass her in person. Carrying the envelope inside, she tossed her purse on the coffee table, sliding a fingernail under the flap of the envelope and drawing out the artfully framed photograph inside. Puzzled, she stared at it in confusion, drawn to the ethereal, unquestionable beauty of it but not recognizing herself in the picture.

For a moment, she simply appreciated the sheer artistic beauty of the photo, the lovely face of the model, the luminescence of the eyes, the poignancy of the expression, and thought to herself that Troy was clearly trying to soften the effects of saddling her with a mermaid tail by showing her that some women looked absolutely stunning in them. Kasey sighed. She already knew some women looked good dressed as mermaids. There was the gorgeous Lorelei for one thing, and this woman, the woman in this picture…her eyes widening, Kasey caught her breath, suddenly realizing why the woman in the photograph looked familiar; it was the woman she had seen that morning in the mirror.

The woman in the picture was every inch a mermaid, beautiful and enigmatic, ethereal and graceful – a mermaid who did not tolerate cheating girlfriends, or mocking exes, a woman who did not lose track of her drawing pencils or ask plastic dinosaur bathroom key holders for advice. A woman with no need of sympathy baked goods from kind hearted pastry chefs, however sweet the gesture. That woman was strong and confident, sure of herself and stunning.

Troy had captured her in the moment just before Cassandra had turned up at the banquet, before her confidence had crumbled, before embarrassment and hurt and memories of betrayal had brought tears to her eyes. In that moment, caught unaware thorough the lens of a dear friend who loved her without reservation, she was every bit as beautiful and confident as Lorelei. For a moment, just a moment, Kasey saw herself as Troy – and maybe even Lorelei – saw her, and it was a revelation. Suddenly, Cassandra's opinion didn't matter any more.

Pushing through the door of Undersea Cottage, Lorelei felt the familiar surge of contentment that always enveloped her as she stepped into her beloved home. Though small and eccentric, the cottage tapped somehow into her inner soul, her creative spirit, welcoming her to a haven of peace and beauty every time she crossed the threshold. Troy's almost maniacal insistence that she purchase the doomed little piece of property a year ago had bordered on the bizarre, but Lorelei knew him well enough to understand that the cottage – a one of a kind structure that had started life as a run of the mill bungalow – had captured his heart in a way no other house could have done.

Several months, a bottle of Sauvignon blanc, and a long heart to heart discussion later, he had admitted over a plate of Spanish tomato toast with garlic and olive oil, that the artist/architect who had transformed the little house from average to enchanting, was none other than Matteo Fabiano, the man who had taken Troy's heart with him when he passed away two years before. The renovation, commissioned by the then owners of the property, had been the homeowner's idea, but the creation of the magical underwater rooms and hallways had been Matteo Fabiano's vision. Appreciative of, but not overly attached to Undersea Cottage while Matteo was living, Troy had become obsessively invested in it after the death of his lover and had badgered the owners for the listing the moment he heard they were looking to sell.

The provision in the bill of sale addendum to the deed prohibiting the dismantling of the ocean themed art installations had been added at Troy's insistence, but the owners of the cottage, eager to leave Indiana and retire to Florida, had agreed to remove the stipulation the moment the first prospective buyers made an offer. Unable to afford to purchase the cottage himself at the time, Troy had immediately put his condo on the market to raise the money, but time had run out before he could raise the funds to save the cottage and the art installations it contained. Lying baldly, he had told the prospective buyers that the property had already been sold, risking his job on the falsehood as he desperately began making phone calls, starting with Lorelei. Fortunately for Troy, she had fallen in love with the little house the moment she saw it.

Thinking back to that long ago conversation and the pile of paperwork it had engendered, Lorelei felt a pang of emotion that had nothing to do with Undersea Cottage or the real estate office where Troy had worked at the time. It was the first and only time she had ever seen her friend on the verge of tears. If Troy had asked her to purchase a four story time share dog house on the dark side of the moon, she would have done it without hesitation, just to drive the pain from the blue of his eyes. It had been heartbreaking.

Pausing in the doorway, she dropped her keys into the patchwork fabric purse slung over her shoulder, bending to pick up a tissue wrapped package that had clearly been slipped through the heavy, hinged, cast iron sea shell mail slot in the front door. Drawing the ribbon and paper free, she sank onto the comfortable sofa in the center of the living room and tucked a soft velvet sea anemone and a lace trimmed grey pillow shaped like an oyster behind her back. Dropping the paper to the ocean floor texture of the floorboards, she turned over the ornate little frame gilded in faux gold leaf.

Staring back at her from the frame was an enchanting photo of Kasey taken at the banquet, her features exquisite, her eyes luminous, her artfully arranged hair a nimbus of graceful curls surrounding her face. That the curls had been achieved with a hot curling iron and half a can of ultra hold and the luminous eyes reflected the light of a dozen or more prismed chandeliers made no difference. In that moment, all that beauty had belonged to Kasey, and she had owned every second of it.

Unaware but vaguely suspecting that Troy (switching tactics to employ a dual prong assault) had hand delivered the enticing picture as a none too subtle nudge in the direction of romantic assignations, she rose, abandoning her shoes once again to pad barefoot through the dreamy half light of the underwater landscape, hanging both the little gold frame and the portrait from the coffee shop on the wall above the curving plaster shell that was the fireplace mantel. Drawing the eye and reflecting the subtle colors of the sea glass embedded in the hearth and the curling sea grasses of the wrought iron fire screen, the two pictures looked as though they had been created for the express purpose of being the finishing pieces of a predestined puzzle.

Shaking her head at the dramatic overtones of the thought – living in an underwater environment made one prone to dreamy interpretations, she mused wryly – Lorelei returned to the sofa and her pillows, reaching for the cell phone she had forgotten on the table. If Kasey had not called her back, she decided with sudden resolution, she would call her again.

Nodding in absentia to Troy, who she knew would not give up until she and Kasey were neck deep in either ruin or romance, she slid her index finger across the lock screen, delighted to see that someone – Kasey Martin? – had left her a message. Thumbing the phone into speaker mode, she smiled as Kasey's voice, rushed and flustered as though trying to leave the message before losing her nerve, rose from the tiny cell phone speaker in her hand.

"Hi, Lorelei. It's me. It's Kasey, I mean, calling you back. On my phone. Obviously on my phone, I... um, I just wanted to call to tell you that I would like to take you up on your invitation, and to ask you if you drink coffee. I mean, of course you probably drink coffee. But I wondered if you would like to do it. With me." The message paused for a moment, a rush of recorded air playing back a sudden mortified gasp, as Kasey realized what she had said. "Drink coffee with me, I meant, not do it with me! Not that I wouldn't, I mean not that you might, that...I'm just making this worse, aren't I?" A second pause sounded, and Lorelei could imagine the other woman taking a deep breath, her sweet face impossibly flustered, closing her eyes in concentration and forcibly pulling herself together. A moment later, Kasey's message continued. "Anyway, if you would like to take me out for coffee, I would very much like for you to take me. Or I could take you. Out! For coffee! Oh god, I'm hanging up now."

The message, a certified disaster of stumbling suggestions and accidental double entendre, was clearly impossibly mortifying. Lorelei had never heard anything so adorable in her life. Turning her eyes to the paper she had hung over the mantel, she wondered what Kasey would make of the mysterious portrait and decided to ask her.

Chapter Twelve

When Lorelei returned Kasey's call that afternoon, Kasey had just finished removing the last traces of wine and humiliation from her cell phone and had settled down in a comfortable position on the sofa to panic about the missing portrait. Consoling herself that the lost piece of paper could have been found by anybody (gallery owner? Wealthy patron? Impressed art critic for the local paper?) just as easily as it might have been found by Lorelei, she tried to ignore the mortifying possibility that the free spirited beauty whose essence she had been attempting to capture with paper, graphite and colored pencils might now consider her a dangerous stalker. Or at the very least a pathetic local girl with a crush. Eyes widening suddenly, she tried to remember whether she had signed the bottom of the portrait, but backed away from that dark maw of possibility quickly before she could fall in.

Staring at the phone, half afraid that it would ring and half afraid that it wouldn't, she shook her head at her innate ability to take the simplest situation and complicate it beyond all reasonable measure. It had been a simple if embarrassing gig at a corporate themed banquet, but she had managed to encounter Cassandra and her elegant new girlfriend, completely fail to murder Troy, and fall on her face in front of Lorelei. It had been a simple afternoon in the coffee shop, but she had managed to flee like a startled bird, reaching new heights (or depths?) of cowardice in the process. It had been a simple voice mail with an invitation to go out for drinks or dinner, but she had managed to leave a return message so embarrassing and accidentally inappropriate that she could picture the beautiful Lorelei laughing about it hysterically behind her back with Troy.

Sternly, she mentally shook herself. She knew that was the embarrassment talking; she didn't really believe that. Lorelei had been sweet and concerned, friendly and forthright – she did not seem like the type to mock another person in extremity. And Troy? She knew beyond the shadow of a single doubt that Troy would take a shoe to anyone who spoke a single unkind word against her, and he was a dead shot with a tasseled Ferragamo loafer.

Taking solace in Jorge's now crumbled but well meant pity pastry, Kasey took a moment to fortify herself with the fact that Lorelei had asked her out in the first place, and cradled the now sanitized cell phone against her chest like an adorable but potentially hissing, spitting kitten. When the ring tone went off she nearly leapt out of her skin. Brushing the pad of her index finger across the screen, she could not help but smile when Lorelei's name appeared. Taking a deep breath, she answered the call.

"H-hello?" she said timidly, staring at the photo that Troy had shoved through the mail slot and trying to believe she really was that person. "Lorelei? How are you?"

Later that night, after the phone call had ended and arrangements had been made to meet at a quaint local restaurant the following evening, Kasey drifted from her cramped living room into her tiny bedroom, wearing only an oversized Van Gogh Starry Night T Shirt and a sweet, blissful smile. As she crawled into bed and drew the blanket over her shoulders, the persistent sound of her arguing neighbors rose beyond the bedroom wall, its cadence loud, familiar and usually irritating. This, time Kasey did not care. This time she fell asleep smiling.

Across town, ensconced in the dreamy, artistically embellished confines of Undersea Cottage, Lorelei lay curled on the pale green sofa, staring at the pencil portrait pinned up above the mantel, and the photograph of Kasey in the gilded frame. She fell asleep smiling too.

Chapter Thirteen

The little restaurant where Lorelei and Kasey met for dinner stood on the edge of a lake too small to appear on the official google map of lakes and rivers in Indiana, but large enough to attract serenading crickets, gracefully floating wild ducks and geese and the reflection of the moon. Sitting on an outdoor terrace, the balmy breezes of late summer caressing their skin, the two women made an irresistibly pretty picture, flickering light from the jar candle on the table between them painting dancing shadows across their faces.

"So," said Lorelei, relaxed and comfortable in her skin as always, "how long have you been an actress?"

Also relaxed and comfortable – though her current state had to, in all fairness, be attributed to the half empty bottle of wine on the table – Kasey smiled.

"Well, if you can count lying on a seafood table wearing a mermaid tail as acting, my career is about six years old."

Her forehead creased suddenly, a tiny wrinkle of worry appearing on the smooth skin between her eyebrows. "Oh! But you were a mermaid at the party too! I didn't mean to imply that…"

Laughing, Lorelei shook her head and poured her another glass of wine. "Well it isn't Shakespeare," she conceded, sipping from her own glass and smiling across the table. "But some things you just do because you feel compelled to do them by an irresistible universal force that relentlessly guides your unwilling footsteps toward a higher calling."

Bursting into laughter, Kasey reached for her wine glass as their eyes met in perfect understanding.

"Troy," they both said at the same time.

The observation – wry and true and clearly a shared experience, occasioned another bout of giggling, and at a nearby table, an elderly couple smiled at the sound, taking one another's hands beneath the moonlight and remembering their own, long since passed, days of courting.

"I studied theatre at the university," Kasey offered after a moment, no need to identify by name the campus that for years had formed and then informed the town of Bloomington Indiana. "Dance, music, voice, all the usual things."

Lorelei was delighted. "You sing too? So do I!" she said brightly, though she had to admit, if only to herself, that the sort of duet she found herself contemplating with Kasey Martin did not involve sheet music, notes or lyrics. Tempo, rhythm, crescendo, yes, yes indeed, but not sheet music, notes or lyrics. Sighing unconsciously, she drank in the sight of the moonlight and candlelight dancing together across the creamy duskiness of Kasey's olive skin, and the flickering of the flame in her dark eyes. The woman was a symphony.

Equally captivated, Kasey found herself staring at Lorelei, thinking distractedly of the lost and missing portrait she had drawn, certain now that she could not possibly have captured the luminescent beauty of the woman across the table. Wide green eyes, as mysterious as the depths of the ocean, watched her from underneath long lashes, bright and knowing, as if seeking sunken treasure that only she could tell was there. Drawn into those eyes, willingly drowning, Kasey found herself thinking that for the first time, the old song about the Lorelei made sense. She had always been skeptical, scornful, of the idea that sailors – men, obviously – would allow themselves to be wrecked upon the rocks, dragged beneath the waves, lost irretrievably at sea never to return, all for the beauty of a woman. In that moment, she admitted to herself that for one kiss from those lips, lush, inviting and currently smiling, she would abandon ship a thousand miles from land. Feeling the waters closing over her head, she cast about desperately for a point of conversation (what had they been talking about before she fell into those enigmatic eyes?) and drew a desperate headline from the newspaper that morning.

"Have you ever done a show at the Belleview theatre?" she said suddenly, feeling the riptide receding and wondering at the fact that she still felt the urge to hurl herself in the path of a tsunami. "I saw in the paper today that it's going up for final sale."

Lorelei's expression, contented and dreamy as she stared at Kasey, suddenly fell. "I love that theatre!" she cried softly, the faint exclamation more lamentation than confession. "I heard that a huge corporation wants to buy it and tear it down and build another high rise."

Kasey's face, suddenly equally mournful, mirrored Lorelei's. "Where will the ghosts go?" she found herself saying, flushing suddenly at the probability that Lorelei would find such a statement naïve and childish.

Lorelei did not. "I wondered that too when I saw the article this morning. Everyone knows that theatre is haunted. I've done shows there before, back before the renovation, and I've seen some pretty strange things, I can tell you that."

The renovation she was referencing, a complete overhaul of the theatre that had first opened back when vaudeville was in its heyday, had been the talk of the town when it was commissioned. The original theatre, an unassuming if historical half block of bricks and mortar and faded red carpet, had once belonged to the city of Bloomington, but had been sold to a private investor, and - no longer grandfathered into older building and safety codes and specifications – faced significant renovations before it could be reopened.

Transformed by vision, talent and an ostentatious amount of money, the building had left its humble roots behind, and become a dazzling vintage style venue worthy of Pavarotti or Josephine Baker, or Billie Holiday in their heyday. Kasey, too, had done locally produced shows at the theatre in the past, and could not believe the pictures which had emerged of the architectural transformation. Three weeks away from a grand reopening with a red carpet, special guests and visiting luminaries, the theatre was suddenly boarded up, an alarm system installed, and its ornate, new front doors padlocked. Mysterious renovations continued on the upper floors, then – with no explanation whatsoever – the light in the upper story windows went dark, and the heavily padlocked doors began gathering dust. Some time later, in the absence of a legally represented owner, the building had reverted to the city once again, and had recently been put up for sale at auction, victim to the popularity of the shiny new theatre the city had built three blocks over on fifth street. Unwilling, or unable, to support the operating costs and upkeep on the renovated building, the city was selling it to raise funds for a much needed parking garage in the downtown area. What the new owners would do with the valuable property on which the theatre was situated was anybody's guess.

A "Save the Belleview Theatre" grassroots project had gained some traction in the earlier months of the year when the impending sale was first announced, but when the amount of money projected to be necessary to purchase the property was revealed, even the hardiest of local historical and theatre activists had quailed at the enormity of the effort, and gone down almost without a fight. It had broken Kasey's heart.

"There's an open house down there tomorrow," Lorelei said suddenly, driven to banish the wistful sadness from the eyes of the lovely woman in front of her. "Would you like to go? I would love to see the renovation in person, I heard it was spectacular. I mean, the open house is for prospective buyers, of course, but we could go. Open house means open doors, doesn't it? We could dress to the nines and carry briefcases and pretend to be investors." Her smile – already encouraging – became wickedly mischievous. "what do you say?"

Kasey returned the smile with equal delight. "I say, bring on the briefcases."

Feeling a sudden rush of delight from the top of her head to her toes, Lorelei grinned. She had never found any woman quite bold enough to leap feet first alongside of her into whatever whimsical mischief she envisioned, at least not without hesitation, skepticism and a rapidly fading enthusiasm. Kasey looked as if she was all in, all about it and up for anything. Bending to draw the keys to Undersea Cottage from the purse resting on the floor at her feet, Lorelei reached for Kasey's hand. "Will you come home with me?" she said, now certain there was a mutual connection between them. "There is something I want to show you."

Chapter Fourteen

When Kasey entered Undersea Cottage for the first time, she was captivated, enchanted, and utterly delighted. Running a slender finger along the delicate tracery of the sea grasses painted faintly on the walls, she let out a long, slow breath, her artist's heart rejoicing in the textured finishes, the twisting, coral reef like columns, the stained glass windows. Fashioned in ocean colors, the tall windows were framed in pale, sheer curtains dyed in greens and blues that faintly tinted the light streaming in from outside, casting moving shadows of colored sunlight against trompe l'oeil floorboards painted to look like the bottom of the ocean.

In patches that blended seamlessly with faint, delicate watercolor murals of sea life, sections of the wall were stenciled in faint, barely there patterns suggesting scales, edged in the faintest brush of clear and luminescent glitter, creating an effect of muted natural bioluminescence. Kasey had never seen anything so beautiful.

Drifting from room to room of the little cottage like a sea creature impelled by the tide, she pressed her hand to wavy blue green glass set into the curve of a spiral stairwell leading to the second floor, its wrought iron railing reminiscent of the ribs of a long forgotten shipwreck, its stairs embedded with spiral shell fragments and smooth sided pebbles, wave washed sea glass and fossil like impressions of sea creatures long forgotten by marine biologists and modern aquariums.

Above the highest point of the staircase, moving faintly in the currents from hidden air conditioner venting, an ethereal kinetic sculpture hovered gracefully, affixed to the ceiling but seemingly free floating; gossamer strips of translucent fabric, filmy and diaphanous, suggesting a jelly fish like sea creature animated by water. Kasey felt her heart catch at the beauty of it and turned to say so, freezing in her tracks as her eyes fell onto the pencil portrait hanging above the shell shaped fireplace mantel. She suddenly found she could not breathe.

Misinterpreting her expression, Lorelei hurried across the room. "Okay, I know it's kind of weird, all the fish and shells and sea plants and stuff, but I love this place, honestly. I never want to move away." She paused at the foot of the staircase. "It was designed by the same artist who did the theatre renovation," she explained, as Kasey stepped off of the curving treads of the staircase and down into the living room, "so I thought you might like to see it."

Shaking her head and forcing herself to breathe again, Kasey was quick to correct her misapprehension. Assuring Lorelei that she thought the cottage was stunning and extraordinary, she took a step away from the incriminating piece of paper pinned to the wall, but froze in her steps a second time when she noticed her own picture, dressed as a mermaid, hanging just below the portrait on the wall. Following her gaze to the framed photograph, Lorelei flushed.

"Troy," she said, gesturing toward the photo, as if that were explanation enough. It was.

Relaxing infinitesimally when Lorelei did not mention the pencil portrait, Kasey nodded. "He sent me one too," she murmured. "I wonder what he's up to."

Stepping closer, her eyes never leaving Kasey's face, Lorelei lifted a gentle finger to brush aside a stray strand of long, sleek hair, feeling a strange fluttering in her chest when her fingertip brushed against the warm silk of Kasey's cheek. For a moment she was inclined to believe that the magic of the moment was the product of the underwater environment, the liquid aspect of the reflected colors, the sinuous, almost seductive dance of the kinetic sculpture, and the shadows it threw over Kasey's features. In the next moment, their lips meeting in a gentle but heated consummation of the moment, she realized she was wrong.

Surprised by a trembling that seemed to rise inside her and grow with every passing moment of Lorelei's lips on hers, Kasey closed her eyes and melted against the soft body that pressed against hers, the gentle arms that supported her when her knees grew suddenly weak, the sweet perfume of lavender and roses that seemed to curl from Lorelei's skin and hair like some subtle alchemy of desire, drawing her to give in, to release her doubts, her fears, her determination to resist ever again trusting her heart to another person.

Overcome by the sensation, Kasey once again felt as if she were drowning but had no desire to save herself. Cassandra had certainly never kissed her like that. No one ever had. Caught up in a surge of something she could never have described in the moment, Kasey gave in to the thrill that flooded through her, returning the kiss with every ounce of passion and glory she kept hidden beneath the quiet façade she always showed to the world. Lorelei was swept away by it; they both were.

The rush in her blood rising to a thrumming pitch, Lorelei drew Kasey closer, scarcely aware of the movement, of the motion, feeling as if the moment were magical and nearly prophetic. This was no ordinary first kiss, no ordinary beginning, no ordinary meeting of hearts and bodies. She would have staked her life on it. In her arms, Kasey seemed to come alive, surging to meet her like waves on the shoreline, ebbing and flowing but never losing the rhythm of the tide. Her heartbeat, thudding faster against the heat of Lorelei's breast, rose in pitch and in ferocity until it sounded in her ears like thunder, and it was a long moment – intense and wild for both of them – before they realized that the thunder they were hearing was not the rhythm of their combined heartbeats, but somebody pounding on the door.

Breaking the kiss, reluctantly but necessarily, Lorelei let her arms fall from around Kasey, but caught the other woman's hand as she moved to cross the living room floor, unwilling to break physical contact with her, or leave her side despite the summons. Flushed and disheveled, a secret heat and knowing in both of their eyes, they approached the door together and stepped back as Lorelei swung it open. A moment later, both of them forgot everything that had just happened.

Standing in the doorway, neither steady on his feet nor sober, Troy stood swaying as though a brisk wind might actually blow him over. Clutching an expensive and nearly empty bottle, his Italian silk tie unknotted and askew, his fastidious suit wilted and rumpled, he stared at them in silence for a moment, his handsome, familiar face pale and dark, unshaven stubble covering the skin that was tight and drawn over his angled jaw and high, aristocratic cheekbones. His empty fist, the one not holding the bottle, was clenched in helpless anguish, his lips pressed together as if to keep from speaking, and his blotched face and red eyes made it clear that he had – in the moments before his arrival – actually been crying. Neither Kasey nor Lorelei had ever seen him in such a state. It was utterly terrifying.

Chapter Fifteen

"You are in no condition to be driving," Lorelei scolded quietly, sinking down on the sofa beside Troy and hiding her desperate worry behind the words as she pressed a cool compress to his face and pulled the silk tie out from his collar to open his top shirt button. "What were you thinking?"

"I wasn't thinking," Troy muttered from under the cool, damp washcloth, his voice muted by a barricade of terry cloth fibers. "I'm not."

Sinking down on the sofa on the other side of him, Kasey seized his ankles and lifted his legs to a nearby leather ottoman shaped like a turtle carapace, easing the designer shoes he wore off his feet and resting a comforting hand on one of his fancy dress socks.

"Troy," she begged quietly, horrified that he had gotten behind the wheel of his vintage sports car and desperately relieved that he had arrived at the cottage in one piece. "What happened?"

Sliding the cloth down his face with a slow, miserable movement, Troy hung his head, acknowledging that he had executed a dangerous lapse in judgement, but too wretched in the moment to say so. He could not seem to care that he had endangered himself by driving while intoxicated, but if he had caused harm to anyone else by driving in his condition, they all knew that he would never have forgiven himself. He did not seem surprised to find the two of them together.

"You already know that they are selling the Belleview theatre," he said, his voice muffled by misery and fresh tears threatening at the corners of his eyes, though he refused to let them fall. "It was supposed to be sold at auction the day after tomorrow, but I just found out that they already have a buyer and aren't opening the auction to the public at all." His expression twisted bitterly. "They have a corporate purchaser ready to hand over the money – looking to build a new office block. They only want the property, they aren't going to save the building at all. The entire renovation, all the art – the statues, the murals, the mosaics – everything, they're just going to destroy it." He sat up and lowered his feet to the floor, resting his elbows on his knees and burying his face in his hands. "Everything Matteo created, smashed and ground into rubble and carted away."

Kasey raised a horrified eyebrow. "Matteo?" she echoed, as Lorelei made sympathetic noises and continued rubbing Troy's rumpled shoulder with gentle fingers. "Your Matteo?"

Kasey shook her head, stunned to learn that Troy's lost love, the mysterious architectural artist, had been the creative genius behind not only the magnificent theatre renovation, but behind Undersea Cottage as well.

Shaking his own head, the gesture bitter and defeated, Troy raised his hands in a helpless, empty gesture. "They're going to wreck it," he said, his fingers curling into unconscious fists again, as though he could find those he deemed responsible and take revenge for what they were planning to do to the precious memory of his lost love. "They're going to raze it, level it, wipe it out," he muttered. "Pave paradise and put up a parking lot." He hummed the old song tunelessly for a moment, morose and miserable, then reached again for the bottle. Lorelei carefully moved it out of his reach.

"They are going to take Matteo's last great work, his masterpiece, his magnum opus," he said, grief and mourning painting lines on his face where before no lines had existed, "and they are going to destroy it."

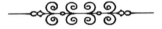

Pouring Troy into the back seat of the battered old Nissan, Kasey drove in silence across town, glancing in the rearview mirror every few seconds to check on her friend. Sprawled across the back seat, his posture as untidy as his clothing, he didn't even look like Troy. Following behind them, cautious and careful in Troy's expensively restored powder blue nineteen fifty six Mercedes convertible, Lorelei worried.

The ascent to the fifth floor that housed Troy's condo was aided considerably by the wood paneled, graciously carpeted elevator, and Kasey and Lorelei half carried him down the elegant hallway toward his front door with one of his arms over each of their shoulders. Usually meticulous and fastidious to a fault, he smelled like sadness, fine cologne and alcohol, and stumbled to bed leaving a trail of discarded clothing behind him on the imported Aubusson carpet. Burying his face in sheets of fifteen hundred thread count Egyptian cotton, he hid from his grief in shirtsleeves and dress pants, his shoes abandoned at the foot of the bed, his jacket cast off in the living room hallway. For a moment, he lay as if dead.

Reaching for the switch that operated the elegant track lighting he had installed the week he moved in, Lorelei paused as a faint sound rose from the bedclothes, and Troy turned a sorrowful face to the light for just a moment.

"The candle," he murmured quietly, and Lorelei shushed him gently.

"I know, I know," she said tenderly, brushing a disheveled lock of hair away from his forehead and planting a kiss in its place. "Don't worry. I'll take care of it."

Turning from the bed, she drew a small, fresh candle from the top dresser drawer and lit it from the sputtering wick of the candle already burning in the holder in front of Matteo's picture. Setting it aside, the flame preserved, she blew out the original candle and, waiting just long enough for the wax to cool, she replaced it with the new one. Seeing this sacred task accomplished safely, Troy closed his red rimmed eyes at last, and was sound asleep in seconds

Kasey blinked back tears. "He's breaking my heart," she murmured to Lorelei, drawing the blankets of the bed up over him and tucking them carefully around his shoulders.

"I know," Lorelei whispered, turning out the lights and following Kasey through the bedroom door, closing it quietly behind them. "He's breaking my heart too."

"I had no idea that Troy's Matteo was the man responsible for the renovation of the Belleview theatre," Kasey said, keeping her voice low even though she doubted that Troy would be awakened by anything less than an explosion. It was clear that their friend had taken refuge from his turmoil, first in alcohol and now in sleep, and she did not think it kind to deny him that.

"The Belleview theatre and my house," Lorelei answered, rummaging in Troy's high tech refrigerator for a predictably artsy craft beer and in a neatly organized drawer for a bottle opener. "Do you want one?"

Nodding, Kasey sank down on the black leather sofa and shoved several small throw pillows—elegant dove grey with black piping—to one side.

Clearly comfortable and familiar with the contents of Troy's condo and cupboards, Lorelei returned from the spotless kitchen, opening the second beer bottle and handing it to Kasey.

"Don't you ever tell Troy we drank these out of the bottle instead of a pilsner glass," she warned, settling onto the other end of the sofa. "He'll have a conniption fit."

Smiling at the thought of the impeccable Troy Preston ever having anything so untidy as a conniption fit (whatever that actually was), Kasey sobered quickly, remembering the state in which they had just driven him home.

"You don't have to stay," Lorelei said suddenly, "this can't be much fun for you." She glanced over one shoulder at the closed bedroom door, but the room beyond it was silent. "I'll stay here and sleep on the sofa – just in case he needs anything. I don't want him to wake up and be alone."

"You're a good friend," Kasey said quietly, drawn to move closer to her on the sofa. "I'm glad that he has you."

Lorelei smiled fondly. "I'm glad he has you too," she answered, smiling as Kasey's subtle movement brought their knees in contact. "But I wanted to take you out for a nice dinner, maybe home for a night cap – instead you got caught up in an intervention and a rescue."

"I would do anything for Troy," Kasey said, her voice suddenly serious, her expression intense. "I hope that you know that."

For a moment, Lorelei studied Kasey, one hand rising to brush against the smooth skin of her cheek for a moment before falling back to her lap.

"Troy won't admit it," she said suddenly, rising to rummage once again in her friend's gourmet kitchen, "but he's got boxes of microwave popcorn hidden under the sink, and like a hundred cable channels. We can have a slumber party." Her head popped out from behind the open cupboard door. "If you want to, I mean."

Smiling, suddenly as relaxed and comfortable as if she had known Lorelei forever, Kasey nodded, reaching for the slender, streamlined remote resting in an embossed tray on a tufted leather ottoman.

"That sounds wonderful," she said, realizing she meant it. "There's always some channel playing Casablanca at any given moment. Do you like old movies?"

Emerging from the kitchen with bags of popcorn and a collection of fancy nuts, stone ground crackers and gourmet cheeses, Lorelei grinned delightedly, and raised a saucy eyebrow.

"Here's looking at you, kid," she answered.

When Troy emerged from his bedroom the following morning, he found Kasey and Lorelei curled together amid scattered throw pillows, fingers linked, limbs intertwined, sound asleep and smiling. Kasey's cheek was pillowed on Lorelei's shoulder, Lorelei's chin rested on top of Kasey's head, and on the television was the old black and white movie that had been playing on repeat all night. Smiling, Troy reached for the remote and clicked off the flat screen.

"Casablanca," he murmured, setting the remote back on the embossed tray where it belonged. "Does it every time."

Collecting the empty craft beer bottles with a scandalized expression at the lack of appropriate drinking receptacles, he moved silently toward the kitchen and opened the door that hid the trash bin, dropping the bottles together into the bag with a loud and resounding crash. Startled awake by the sound, both Lorelei and Kasey sat up quickly on the cushions.

Posed artfully in the doorway, Troy nodded in greeting, shaved and styled and dressed to the nines, from the top of his perfectly coiffed head to the soles of his perfectly shined shoes. Gone were all traces of the emotional wreck he had been the night before; if anything, he seemed filled with new and dangerous purpose.

"Well what have we here," he purred without acknowledging the events of the night before. "Two lovebirds on my loveseat?" Smiling slyly, he retrieved his car keys from the small round marble topped table near the door where Lorelei had left them, tossed them in the air and caught them expertly. "I will trust you ladies to see yourselves out," he said airily, stepping to the door and pulling it closed behind him. "I have places to go and I have things to do. I love you, my darlings, help yourselves to breakfast."

With that he was gone, and Kasey and Lorelei stared at each other in confusion at his apparent spontaneous rehabilitation.

Shaking her head, Lorelei pushed aside the tumble of throw pillows.

"What on earth just happened?"

Chapter Sixteen

After divesting Troy's refrigerator of a breakfast equal parts gourmet offerings and opportunistic foraging, Lorelei looked at Kasey in sudden realization and shrugged helplessly.

"Can I get a ride home with you? Troy took his car."

Deciding to follow through with their plan to visit the theatre since it would likely be their last chance, Lorelei and Kasey each returned home to take advantage of toothbrushes and fresh clothing, meeting in the parking lot a block from the theatre building just before lunch time. There had been no word from Troy.

Entering the building through the wide double doors at the front, they paused in the middle of the ornate and sumptuous lobby, each of them reaching for a slickly printed and glossy pamphlet from a pile on a carved wooden table to one side of the door. Describing the theatre, its history in the community, and the phenomenal refurbishing done by the late artist Matteo Fabiano, the brochures had been lovingly produced by the local historical society, awaiting a ribbon cutting ceremony and grand reopening that it now seemed was never going to happen.

Opening the shiny paged booklet to the back cover, Kasey stared at the photograph of Matteo Fabiano, captivated by the chiseled jaw, the handsome features, and the light that gleamed in his eyes as he surveyed the building into which he had poured his art, his heart and his talent. Surrounded by his paintings, his sculptures and the fruits of his labors, his expression glowed with an intensity that seemed to captivate the camera, glorying in the beauty of his creation without a trace of arrogance or prideful posturing. His was the face of the quintessential artist, drawing beauty from thin air and fashioning it into something tangible, knowing as he did that in doing so, he was answering the summons of a holy calling. He had lived doing exactly what he had been born to do, and he had died far too soon, while still doing it.

"No wonder Troy loved him," Kasey murmured, her elbow brushing against Lorelei's as she held the picture to the light. "He was exquisite." She did not mean Matteo's handsome face or lean body, his soulful eyes or noble forehead, and Lorelei knew it.

"He was extraordinary," she said, gesturing around the empty lobby of the theatre. "I mean, look at this place."

Soaring high above them, several stories over their heads, the ceiling of the entry lobby glowed with what looked to be the last dying echoes of sunset in a faux night sky of deep cobalt blue streaked with faint lavender and purple. Stepping from the entryway—a sumptuous jewel of gilded architectural elements, opulent marble and velvet, spiraling columns painted in green and crème, and coffered ceilings painted richly in red and gold and blue—they stepped into the illusion of a Mediterranean courtyard, with massive textured paving stones beneath their feet, and what appeared to be the outer walls and roofs of classic, red tiled buildings surrounding them.

From the edges of the rooftops and at the foot of a curving, ornate staircase, sculpted gargoyles peered from behind soaring buttresses and lifted elevated stained glass lanterns bearing cleverly wired light bulbs that mimicked flickering flames, or burning gaslight.

Crossing the gilded courtyard, they entered the palatial main lobby—labelled "Grand Salon" in ornate, gold edged letters—where an opulent concession stand stood in solitary splendor, as if waiting to offer wine and spirits to elegant theatre goers in glittering evening gowns and formal tuxedos. Caught up in the splendor of the building, her artist's heart soaking up every sumptuous detail, Kasey drew a shaky breath and rested one hand on the curving brass railing that surrounded a spectacularly cast fountain, empty now of everything but echoes. Closing her eyes for a moment, she could almost hear the tumble and splash of the water that ought to have filled it, the falling drops a measured symphony heralding a rebirth that had never come to fruition.

Moving in awestruck silence through arched entryways guarded by classical sculptures carved in stone and marble, they reverently stepped into the theatre itself, unable to recognize what had once been a large and serviceable but unambitious auditorium providing a home to touring casts and local theatre productions and summer stock companies of popular Broadway musicals.

In the main room of the spectacularly transformed theatre, where a great stage dominated one end of the massive space, the twilight horizon effect of the ceiling opened out into a full night sky, replete with a whispering hint of moonlight, and stars in breathtaking constellations that were wired to flicker faintly against the velvet blanket of dark sky that surrounded them. Stepping into a small alcove set into the lushly wallpapered walls beneath the mezzanine, they gazed across rows of lushly upholstered seats toward the performance area, which was surrounded by life sized walls and balconies, tiled roofs and curving archways, as if a splendid Mediterranean mansion had opened its luxurious arms and embraced the polished wood boards of the stage, offering inclusion in its own lush opulence and lavish artifice.

The façade, a glorious study in gold gilt, marble block and mosaic tile, was absolutely breathtaking. The enchantment that had brought whimsy to sweet little Undersea Cottage had been given full reign in this echoing, cavernous space, and the illusion of a magical night in an exotic, beautiful, foreign locale was complete and absolute.

If anyone had asked her, Kasey would have sworn that the street outside, the people going about their ordinary lives, the cars and buses and college students of Bloomington, had all ceased to exist, and that the two of them had been swept away through some inexplicable portal to a place of indescribable, impossible beauty. Mesmerized, she found herself thinking that with such a brilliant midnight sky above her, she could make a hundred thousand starlit wishes, but as Lorelei's hand reached for hers in the dark and drew her close in the shadows of the alcove, she realized she had only one wish that in that moment really mattered. As a clever lighting effect caused a single shooting star to cast its path across the glorious ceiling, she closed her eyes, made a wish, and felt that wish come true.

Chapter Seventeen

The kiss that followed under the intimate light of Matteo Fabiano's shimmering stars was like no other kiss Kasey had ever experienced. The tender poignancy of Lorelei's lips on hers might have been heightened by the impossibly romantic atmosphere, by the incredibly gorgeous surroundings, by the sheer beauty of the building that rose on all sides around them like a gilded movie set for the most romantic story in cinematic history…but probably not. It was more likely, as Kasey thought with the very small part of her brain that was still functioning, that two separate and distinctly beating hearts, neither one knowing until now what had been missing inside them all along, had suddenly started beating in tandem.

Deepening the kiss, drawing Kasey closer, Lorelei forgot the fate of the theatre for a moment forgot Troy's strange and inexplicable recovery from his grief of the night before, forgot that she had been planning to ask Kasey's opinion of the mysterious portrait she had found. The only thing she remembered, as accelerated pulses and heightened breathing swept both of them away in a sensuous, exquisite flood of feeling, was that when she had postulated earlier that Kasey's dusky skin would feel like silk beneath her fingers, that it would be like heaven to slide her hands through that long, glossy hair, that the soft curves and patchouli scented limbs that pressed against her, twined around her, would feel like an extension of her own body—she had been right.

"Ahem!"

The sharp clearing of a throat and the audible tapping of an impatient foot broke into their reverie, as a uniformed security guard raised a flashlight and shattered the moment between them.

"Ladies," the woman said wryly, as if annoyed but not shocked to find two women kissing in a velvet curtained alcove. "The open house has been cancelled. I'm going to need to lock up in here."

Flustered and bemused, her pupils dilated and lips slightly swollen from kissing, Kasey stared at her.

"Cancelled?" she echoed, adjusting articles of clothing that had somehow become untucked and partly unbuttoned. "Why?"

She was not at all certain how her green silk blouse and black pencil skirt had become so artfully disarranged in the darkness, but she was certain she had probably enjoyed it. Dazedly, she fished for the string of vintage jet beads that had become lost somewhere in her cleavage, then decided to leave them there and ask Lorelei to help her find them later. Heavens! Kasey shook her head abruptly, taking a sudden and necessary step away from the seductive siren that was Lorelei Desciance. What was the crabby woman in the security uniform saying again?

"The open house has been cancelled," Lorelei murmured out of the corner of her mouth, the blending of her lipstick and Kasey's painting her lips a new and interesting shade of burgundy. "They've already found a buyer for the theatre. Troy told us last night. Remember?"

Kasey remembered, belatedly, her head slowly clearing itself of soft skin, heated lips and tousled, turquoise hair. "Oh yeah, he did," she murmured back, suddenly once again flooded with concern for their friend, and questions about his sudden return to clear thinking and determination after his night of mourning.

Lorelei took her elbow in gentle fingers, steering her out of the auditorium and across the glorious Mediterranean courtyard and sumptuous red velvet draped lobby toward a small door adjacent to the front entrance, where bright sunshine and noisy real life blared from beyond a narrow door marked "Exit".

"Kasey," Lorelei was whispering, as though keeping secrets from the stiff shouldered, straight backed security guard who ushered them out and locked the door behind them. "What do you think happened to Troy? He was so upset last night, and then this morning he left the condo like he was on a mission, as if last night had never happened."

Kasey nodded. "I wonder what he's up to?" she said in innocent and about-to-be-enlightened naivete.

A moment later, they emerged around the corner of the doomed theatre just in time to discover Troy, who – having girded his loins with Italian silk and vintage Versace – was determinedly chaining himself to the front doors of the building.

On the sidewalk in front of the ornately embellished entrance façade, facing off with Troy like two stylish, well groomed pit bulls wearing designer clothing, stood a horrifyingly familiar woman. Swathed from head to foot in a classic Alexander McQueen that probably cost more than either Lorelei or Kasey earned in a year's worth of art shows, theatre roles and toothpaste commercials, Cassandra Carat's well heeled girlfriend (extremely well heeled, her shoes alone cost more than Lorelei's mortgage) stood brandishing a sheaf of papers and a Louis Vuitton briefcase with a tiny golden padlock. Kasey presumed she wore the key to the briefcase on a chain around her neck, resting in the place where her heart was supposed to be.

Lorelei was horrified. "Troy!" she cried, taking in and correctly interpreting the fury on the face of the expensively hired lawyer in front of them. "You can't just chain yourself to the doors of the building!"

Troy smiled fiercely, for a moment seeming a little unhinged. "Well apparently I can, darling," he answered, "because clearly, I have!" His expression sobered for a moment. "Do you think these chains come in anything other than silver? So gauche," he muttered.

"Sir?" The policeman who had been sent from the downtown precinct to deal with the situation seemed at a bit of a loss. "Can I help you?"

Digging in the heels of his imported Italian wingtips, Troy retreated behind a bastion of stubbornness and expensive after shave, looping his elbows through the lengths of chain that wrapped around him and gripping the twin brass doorknobs.

"According to section 5763.003a of the laws governing the disbursement of city owned assets, including real estate, members of the public must be provided fair and equal opportunity to purchase all properties or assets sold by auction or private sale," he pronounced with immense dignity, as Lorelei and Kasey held their breath and wondered how they were going to come up with enough money to bail him out of jail. Troy would not do well in jail, they both knew. He was far too pretty.

"By law," Troy was still holding forth, "as a citizen of this city, I have the right to place a bid on this property." He narrowed his eyes and shot the lawyer a poisonous glower. "There are irregularities in the paperwork," he threatened, "and I am going to find them."

Convinced that Troy had just made up every single syllable of the lecture he was delivering (he had), Kasey glanced at Cassandra's lawyer girlfriend, chilled by the expression filling the other woman's features. Startled, she wondered if there were actually some truth in Troy's ad hoc legal argument, because the beautiful, angry woman had taken a step away from the theatre, staring at him now with open hostility.

"Fine," she snapped, gesturing for the reluctant policeman to put away the handcuffs he had drawn hesitantly from the loop on his belt. "Have your auction, make your bid, go ahead. But I guarantee you that my clients will simply outbid any offer you make to buy the property. You are wasting your time and your efforts," she sneered. "And your chains."

She turned icily to hand the police officer a gold embossed business card. "Reid Monteforte," she said in clipped, angry tones, "of Monteforte, Price, and Riskin." She shot another malevolent expression at Troy, who was muttering *"Dewey, Cheatem and Howe"* under his breath. "Feel free to contact me if there are any further…disturbances once the property has been purchased through my firm."

The policeman nodded, slipping the card into his pocket, taking his leave with obvious relief and striding up the sidewalk to the squad car that was parked at the curb.

"Run along, darling," Troy said sweetly to Reid Monteforte, curling his lip over a set of perfectly white, even teeth. "I wouldn't want to keep you. I'm sure you have lives to destroy and orphans to evict."

The lawyer snarled, deliberate and dangerous, and turned on one excruciatingly expensive Manolo Blahnik stiletto. "As it happens," she glowered, stalking toward the limousine waiting at the corner, "I do."

Chapter Eighteen

"It's perfectly simple, darling," Troy said later that day, with a cagey expression which indicated that it was not perfectly simple at all. "As I told that corporate legal shark outside the theatre, there are irregularities in the paperwork."

He sipped his triple venti half sweet non-fat caramel macchiato in innocent contemplation, returning a tiny glass bottle of rum to his inner pocket without adding it to the cup in coy capitulation to the raised eyebrow and eagle eyes of Lorelei.

"I went to the offices of the city planning commission this morning," he said patiently, shoving the plate of pastries he had just purchased into the center of the table for purposes of equal opportunity consumption. He was trying to butter them up and they knew it. The coffee shop where they sat, six blocks west of *Karma Sumatra* and a million lights years in difference, was flooded with natural light, furnished with faux rustic butcher block tables sanded to a silver patina, and shapely silk ficus trees in profusion.

Sleek and well dressed in a grey suit and patterned tie, Troy was holding court in elegant state, as though he had not just barely escaped incarceration by the proverbial skin of his professionally whitened teeth. He was trying to incite Lorelei and Kasey to join his rebellion against the status quo, because, as he quoted sagely, the status was, as a matter of absolute fact, not quo at all.

Kasey was busy embracing sympathy, still emotional at the realization of what the beautiful theatre meant to Troy, and the memory of his intoxicated grief only the night before. Lorelei was more pragmatic.

"What do you mean, irregularities?" she demanded, availing herself of a raspberry hazelnut torte before Troy could take offense at her query and withdraw his offer of extortion pastries.

Troy assumed a pious expression, stirring his coffee with meticulous sweeps of a pearlescent plastic coffee stir stick. "According to the clerk at the administrative offices," he explained, taking her consumption of the torte as a sign of willingness to be an accessory, "a bill of sale and deed transfer were drawn up for the property nearly three years ago, and according to the computer records, the papers were signed, notarized and filed with the seller's affidavit, but no record of the actual transaction could be found. Though the data entry log said that the records should have been on file, they were not – the files weren't on the server, even though they should have been. A much later entry, filed by a temp who only worked at the office for two days and then disappeared, indicated that the original offer had been rescinded, that the purchaser had backed out of the acquisition, and the entire transaction had been cancelled. But that isn't what the original records indicated." He narrowed shrewd blue eyes over the plate of pastry. "At all."

Choosing a berry liqueur cream filled mini éclair from the platter gilded with confectioner's sugar, he consumed it with relish. Whether enacting a high class 'hair of the dog' strategy or congratulating himself on not having a hangover from the night before was inconclusive. Troy almost never had hangovers; he thought they were crass and untidy.

"Troy," said Kasey hesitantly, intrigued but not wanting to seem insensitive to his grief of the night before. "How could the records be there and not be there at the same time?"

"The records of the real estate transaction are missing," Troy explained patiently, nudging a dark chocolate dusted beignet in the direction of Lorelei, who still looked a little bit skeptical. "The records of the records are not. They were entered into the system at some point originally, that much is documented, but later on, for some probably nefarious reason, somebody deliberately deleted them, and tried to hide the fact that they did it."

Kasey shook her head in confusion, one long, dark lock of hair slipping down over one eye. At the corner of her mouth a faint smudge of powdered sugar clung, and Lorelei smiled when she noticed it, filled with an almost irresistible desire to kiss it away.

"Why would someone delete the records?" Kasey was asking, her fingers drumming on the table in front of her.

"That is the question I will be asking," Troy answered smugly, "when I leave here and go down to the office of records this afternoon."

Lorelei protested, uneasily anticipating more chains and real estate inspired dissention in Troy's not too distant future. He looked entirely seditious. Seditious and stylish. And stubborn.

"You can't just march down there, corner some hapless records clerk and demand information based on a conspiracy theory," she objected. "Do you think they are just going to tell you whatever you want to know?"

Troy was undeterred. "With this face?" he smiled, flashing a pair of irresistible dimples. "Bless you, darling, of course they will!" And they did.

Chapter Nineteen

"I was right," Troy pointed out unnecessarily, lounging across the elegant leather of his sofa without making the posture seem sprawling. The remark was unnecessary because he had been saying it since they walked in the door.

"What did you find out?" Kasey asked avidly, less familiar with the sort of trouble Troy was courting, and thus less trepidatious than Lorelei. She took the iced mineral water Troy handed her and set it down carefully so as not to smudge the glass.

"The papers filed to facilitate the sale of the theatre two years ago have disappeared," he reminded them with appropriate flair and a theatrical eyebrow. "The electronic versions of the papers have been deleted from the records."

He paused to pour from the bottle of champagne he had opened to congratulate himself, and Lorelei returned from the kitchen with an open bottle of beer, stepping sideways to avoid tripping on the heavy chains that lay in a jumble on the pattern of the carpet.

"You might want to put these chains away, Troy," she suggested wryly. "People might get the wrong idea about you."

Troy waggled a suggestive eyebrow, clearly indicating that he found the idea hilarious.

"But what did you find out *today*?" Kasey persisted, as if Troy's life were a slowly unwinding soap opera with far too many commercial breaks. Troy leaned forward, well aware that his audience was in the palm of his hand.

"The signature on the papers indicating the cancellation of the sale," he said, with the finesse of a professional magician, "is a forgery."

He sat back against the fine Corinthian leather of the sofa and beamed proudly.

"And you know this because...?" Lorelei prompted, weighing the probability that he would spin the story out as long as possible and contemplating a second bottle of beer.

Troy could not resist. "Because," he said, indulging in a dramatic gesture with the almost empty champagne glass, "the clerk I spoke to was the son of the original clerk, who retired four days before the signature was dated." He nodded sagely. "We examined the scanned copy of the cancellation papers, and he said he was willing to swear on a stack of Bibles that the signature was not his father's."

"He just told you all this?" Kasey asked in innocent surprise, as Lorelei shook a half reproving, half impressed finger in Troy's direction.

"Of course not," she interpreted correctly, "Troy charmed it out of him." She shook her head in admiration, quite certain that the signature on the paperwork was not the only thing Troy and the hapless, smitten clerk had examined together. It wasn't Troy's fault, she thought reasonably, he couldn't help being irresistible. Not that he tried.

"He smelled nice," Troy protested feebly, though clearly in no way repentant in the matter of seducing answers out of a contracted city employee. "I know Dior for men when I smell it," he added, as if that were reason enough for casual canoodling in the office supply room of the city hall of records. Which it probably was. "I only distracted him for a little while."

"Our tax dollars at work," Lorelei observed drily, resigned to the fact that wherever Troy went, love struck men were bound to follow. She couldn't even blame them – Troy was certifiably adorable. She might even have fallen for the charming rascal herself, she thought with amusement, had she not had a thousand reasons not to. Fortunately for her, being a lesbian was her superpower.

"Why would anyone want to forge a signature cancelling a sale, then eliminate the original records?" Kasey was asking, her thoughtful, analytical approach almost sexier than the adorable fedora currently perched atop her long, dark hair. Almost. Lorelei shook her head, forcing her attention back to the matter at hand.

"Who was the original buyer?" she asked suddenly, pleased to see Kasey nodding her head in agreement. It was gratifying to her to know that their thought processes had subtly aligned with each other, as well as their heartbeats. And their lips. And...other things.

"That," said Troy, pouring himself a second glass of champagne and toasting them with conviction, "is what I intend to find out."

Despite Troy's determination to get to the bottom of the cover up enacted in the office of records, he found his intentions thwarted early the next morning, when the previously helpful (and entirely seducable) clerk from the day before suddenly found himself transferred to a branch office on the other end of town, tied to an ancient old computer and a pile of actual microfiche which would have been better served by being put on display in a historical museum than scanned in to a modern day computer. Slaving away in obscurity entering years old property records into the computerized system, he still smiled whenever he thought about blue eyes, artfully tousled sandy hair and dimples. The clerk regretted nothing.

Who had ordered his abrupt and involuntary transfer (and subsequently enforced it) remained a tantalizing mystery, one Troy was unable this time to uncover under the stubborn adherence to protocols enacted by the newly promoted (and relentlessly straight) man who now occupied the desk in the hall of records. It was not the first time in his life that Troy had met a brick wall, but it was the first time he found himself unable to flirt his way through it. Clearly someone involved in the cover up had been owed a favor, and had called it in.

Chapter Twenty

When Lorelei met Kasey at *Karma Sumatra* the following morning, she found herself standing for a moment in the short hallway that ran between the front and back rooms, the silhouette of her shadow falling across the vintage typewriter and nostalgically quaint 1937 Philco radio ensconced in a recessed niche in the wall. Leaning one shoulder – clad in a soft old denim jacket – against the wall, she tipped her head sideways, the soft turquoise strands of her bobbed hair brushing against her collar.

Shifting her freshly purchased latte to her left hand, she juggled two of Jorge's prescription strength blackberry scones from the crook of her elbow, caught between one step and the next, and hovering in the doorway as though her body were caught in a spider's web of insistence. For a moment, her heart and brain conspired against her, uniting with her body in their refusal to let her do even anything so simple as entering the room without pausing to appreciate the beauty that sat, unaware and unaffected, at the table by the window. For a long moment, she stood and simply stared.

Painted in faint, nearly there shades of red, gold and green by the sunlight that streamed through the stained glass panel hanging in the tall window (the art department of the university provided an endless stream of unusual art pieces and starving artists, and Florence like to support the local creative community) Kasey sat bent over an open sketch pad, a handful of colorful pencils scattered at her elbow, and her graceful fingers curled around a piece of drawing charcoal in a manner that was at the same time utterly natural and unreasonably sexy. Lorelei, who had arrived for their date nearly half an hour early, stole a long, precious moment to stare.

Beneath a chocolate brown vintage felt pork pie hat with a black velvet band, the long, sleek strands of Kasey's hair splayed across one shoulder, cascading like silk over the fabric of the indigo jacket she wore; a gorgeous burst of color in the overhead light that splashed down on her from above. Brow furrowed in concentration, dark eyes fixed and focused, she had given herself over completely to her artwork, intent on line and curve, shadow and perspective, and the smooth, confident strokes that brought whatever she was drawing to life on the paper in front of her. Lorelei felt her heart nearly pause inside her before speeding up again, as though viewing some magnificent natural wonder and marveling at its beauty.

Freed suddenly from the mesmerizing effect of the vision in front of her, she stepped swiftly into the back room of the coffee house, utterly unable to stand another moment observing Kasey from a distance. The desire to gaze into the deep brown of those eyes, to hear the longed for and by now familiar timbre of that quiet voice, to coax a spontaneous, lovely laugh from that delicious, delectable mouth, was overpowering. Irrationally, disconnectedly, reminded by the pencils, she remembered she had wanted to tell Kasey about the beautiful portrait of herself that she had found on the floor in this very room, and ask her opinion on the mystery. She crossed the distance between them as if her feet had wings.

"I wanted to tell you something the other night and I forgot!" she said brightly, setting down the latte and scones, so filled with joy at simply being in Kasey's presence that she forgot to announce her arrival.

Letting out a shriek as an unexpected shadow fell across her drawing paper, Kasey leapt to her feet, her heartbeat accelerating suddenly in surprise, then continuing to speed inside her chest when confronted with bright turquoise hair, sexy curves in well worn denim and a thousand watt smile. The flirty little skirt Lorelei was wearing didn't do anything to slow her pulse rate either.

Flustered, she realized that her paper and pencils had fallen to the floor when she leapt up from the table, and her embarrassed exclamation faded into stunned silence as Lorelei and her flirty little skirt bent over to gather her scattered art supplies and sketches. In all her life, Kasey had never understood the phrase "*her mind went blank*", until now. There was a great deal of skin showing between the top of Lorelei's purple leather boots and the hem of her skirt – a filmy, multi layered confection of greens and blues. So much, in fact, that Kasey found herself thinking ridiculously that if the mermaid had indeed traded her voice to the sea witch for a pair of legs, the witch had gotten the bad end of the bargain.

"Sorry!" Lorelei was laughing, the sound a silvery peal like seaside bells on a far away, romantic shoreline, "I didn't mean to startle you!"

Shaking her head, Kasey blushed so fiercely that the flush staining her cheeks was visible despite her smooth olive complexion.

Lorelei meekly returned a handful of pencils. "I just remembered," she was explaining, as Kasey's brain slowly and reluctantly started working again. "I wanted to tell you about a mystery. I found the most amazing piece of artwork on the floor here the other day! Whoever drew it was utterly fantastic – I've never seen such talent. I…"

Paling suddenly, the becoming blush that painted her cheeks fleeing for safer harbors and leaving her adrift, Kasey drew in a horrified breath, scrabbling to return the scattered loose sheets of drawing paper to the confines of the leather bound sketchbook. She wasn't fast enough.

Rising from a second search and rescue mission underneath the table, Lorelei froze in place beside her, her fingers grasping a sheaf of drawing paper on which simple pencil sketches – filled with beauty and emotion – stared back at her in mute confession, clearly the blueprint for the stunningly beautiful portrait that even now was hanging on the wall of Undersea Cottage. Stunned, she sank into the opposite chair.

"Are…are these your drawings?" she asked the obvious, nearly overcome by sheer appreciation for the woman sitting across from her in an agony of embarrassment.

"I wasn't stalking you, I swear!" Kasey cried, her traitorous blushes returning in full force as she admitted the artistic liberties she had taken without permission. In retrospect, the idea of having asked Lorelei to sign an artist's model release before she started drawing her was as ridiculous as admitting that she had indeed sat in the chair near the white brick fireplace, drawing from memory the beautiful features, the bold spirit, the quintessential personality enshrined in nose and chin, cheeks and jawline, curving mouth and bright eyes. That she had been enchanted after only one brief, embarrassing, disastrous meeting. That she had unconsciously continued to draw the portrait from life even after realizing her subject sat in the same room, seemingly oblivious to her effect on the mere mortals that surrounded her.

That Kasey had fled out the back door and hidden behind the dumpster in the alley was a secret she intended to take to her grave, which she almost hoped would open up and swallow her soon. At least until Lorelei gave up on her obvious creepy artistic weirdness and went home. It was mortifying, and at the same time a revelation. The portrait, she realized suddenly with all of her heart, had even then been a labor of love. Bravely, she forced herself to meet Lorelei's eyes, and found them filled with emotions she was not expecting.

Surprise she could have predicted, concern, wariness, perhaps even nervous speculation. What she saw was none of these things.

"I couldn't help but draw you," she whispered, taking courage from the soft light that filled Lorelei's eyes and lovely features. "You were just so beautiful."

Leaning forward, the loose sheets of drawing paper shushing quietly across the table as they slipped from her fingers, Lorelei raised both hands to Kasey's face, her gaze drinking in the soft skin, the delicate features and anxious expression. In that heartbeat, she decided to despise whoever it was that had put that hesitance, that uncertainty, that self doubt into those deep, luminous eyes. In the next heartbeat, she was kissing those tremulous lips, that hesitant smile, and had decided that she wanted to keep kissing them forever.

"Precious!" The declaration was unexpected and close by, simultaneously smug and delighted, as Troy swanned into the back room of the coffee house in a cloud of I-told-you-so and expensive cologne. He slid into a chair at their table without invitation and beamed at them in satisfaction. "I just knew you'd be adorable together."

Chapter Twenty One

Though well within his rights and the dictates of high fashion to appear suddenly in public simply to show off the fabulous designer suit and shirt he wore, Troy had also arrived with a tantalizing collection of clues and facts and metaphorical breadcrumbs, and a trail he had decided Lorelei needed to follow. There was a woman ("isn't there always a woman?" Troy twinkled at Kasey) who had worked in the department of records two years ago when whatever had happened had happened ("Whatever it actually was, darling," said Troy, "and whatever it was is what we need to find out.")

The woman, a simple data entry clerk with pretentions to greater things, had left her position and returned to college, banking a shiny new degree and a millstone of student loan debt around her neck against the possibility that her career would advance faster the more she educated herself.

"She was right, of course," Troy confided, having discovered that the erstwhile data entry clerk was now working in an office at the state level, overseeing an entire department of her own and privy to information Troy was determined to wrest from her by hook, crook or flirting. Lorelei was not surprised.

"So, go and flirt with her until she swoons at your feet and tells you everything you want to know," she said amusedly, pointing out the obvious strategy for a man of Troy's prodigious charm and twin pernicious dimples.

"Ah, but that won't work, Lorelei my dear, and I will tell you why," Troy said, polishing off Kasey's lemon meringue tartlet and winking outrageously at Jorge for another. Jorge, passing through the room on his return from a clove cigarette and facebook break out back, winked in return, slipping his phone into the back pocket of a pair of fitted black chinos. Fully conscious of how well he looked exiting a room, he entered the dimly lit hallway smiling.

Though nominally straight and harboring no real intention of dating Troy Preston at any point in his life, Jorge had no inhibitions regarding admiring him like fine art. Troy – married to the memory of his lost beloved artist – had no intention of dating Jorge either, so really, where was the harm? The two had had a mutual admiration society for years.

"And coffee, darling!" Troy called after Jorge's retreating back, faithful as ever to Matteo's memory but well aware of a nicely worn pair of black chinos and a handsome young pastry chef when he saw them. Troy was loyal, but he was still breathing after all. Unlike Jorge, Troy knew a great deal about art, *and* he knew what he liked. Not all masterpieces were in frames after all.

"Lorelei," he said suddenly, swiveling back around in his chair and seizing his friend by one hand. "There is simply no point in my flirting with the former lady clerk of the city hall of records because she is not interested in men. She is most definitely of the ladies who admire ladies persuasion, if you know what I mean. Which is why *you* need to go and flirt with her instead of me."

Taken aback, Lorelei cast about the room for another agent to enact Troy's theatrically flirtatious espionage but saw only Kasey across the table, clutching her sketchbook like a life preserver in the face of rising flood waters. Wide eyed and open mouthed, she looked terrified that Troy might assign her an appalling mission next, and inevitably charm her into carrying it out by the utilization of methodically weaponized and strategically applied blue eyes and pouty lips. Troy's pouty lips were legendarily effective – he had slayed Kasey's objections with them before. In some circles it was rumored that he could get total strangers to move metaphorical mountains simply by adopting a lost puppy dog expression and holding it until they capitulated. Lorelei had told Troy before that he should only use his powers for good, but he ignored her with impressive and perfectly executed bonhomie. Kasey had never bothered to try to convince him.

Lacking other options to nominate and unwilling to throw Kasey under the Troy bus, Lorelei sighed and shook her head. "What makes you think that I will be able to get this woman to tell me anything?" she protested half heartedly, knowing full well that she would do any and everything in the world to never again see Troy in the broken hearted misery which had overtaken him several nights before. Cavalier and polished on the surface, always in control and keeping his grief locked away in a gold box of memories, it was the first and only time she had ever seen him lose the grip he held over his mourning and give in to the pain which always ran silently beneath the surface. She would never forget seeing him crumble – her own heart still ached with the memory.

"Oh, but that's the best part!" Troy crowed delightedly, pausing to deliver a one two punch of tousled hair and school boy smile as Jorge arrived to set a tray of sumptuous desserts on the table along with a hand crafted coffee beverage made exactly the way Troy liked it. Jorge reflected the smile back at him and returned to the kitchen with a sassy smirk and an elevated sense of swagger.

"What is the best part?" Kasey asked hesitantly, knowing Troy all too well and not entirely certain she wanted to hear the answer. As it turned out, she did not.

"The woman you need to flirt information out of," Troy grinned in satisfaction at Lorelei, fully prepared to bulldoze her objections, "is your ex! She is sure to still be carrying a torch for you. You can probably get her to tell you anything!"

Horrified, Lorelei glanced at Kasey in consternation while waggling a reproving finger in the face of Troy, who beamed in total and absolute unrepentance.

"Why on earth would Allison Inglis still be carrying a torch for me?" she protested weakly.

Troy flapped a dismissive hand and leaned across the table to kiss her soundly on the cheek, careful to prevent his tasteful paisley tie from falling into the coffee. "Darling, who wouldn't?" he answered.

Chapter Twenty Two

Though far from embracing the questionable ethics of flirting with her ex-girlfriend for information (even for Troy) Lorelei was not surprised to realize that what she really felt uncomfortable with was flirting with another woman – any other woman – when what she really wanted to do was to court Kasey Martin like some old fashioned knight in shining armor, composing ballads to her, showing her that chivalry wasn't really dead after all, and wearing some token of her favor while tilting at metaphorical windmills. Smirking slightly, her lovely face bearing an expression worthy of Troy himself, she decided that the lipstick mark that stained the collar of the T-shirt she had traded for a long, flowing skirt and a spaghetti strap camisole before leaving Undersea Cottage would have to count as a favor of her lady's estimation. Her smile fading as she set out to flirt with the wrong woman entirely, Lorelei straightened her spine and set her shoulders (which did things to the spaghetti strap camisole that Kasey noticed and appreciated.)

Muttering various incarnations of old sayings over and over in rotation ("all's fair in love and war", "any port in a storm", "necessity is the mother of invention," "a bird in the hand is worth two in the…" Oh dear. Never mind that one!) she set the GPS on her phone and drove toward the office at which her ex-girlfriend held court, reminding herself that while the two of them had parted nearly a year earlier, they had – on the whole – parted on good terms.

Not wanting the same things out of life was hardly a thing to blame one another for, and – Lorelei thought with an unexpected swelling in her chest – she certainly was not going to resent either Allison or the break up, because if things had not ended as they did, with each of them going their separate ways, she would not have just left Kasey curled up on the sofa at Undersea Cottage, smiling and sleeping, a green and blue crocheted blanket tucked over her, her shoes tossed on the trompe l'oeil sandy ocean floor and her lipstick smudged from kissing. Kasey had not liked the idea of ex-girlfriend flirtation as a strategy, Lorelei could tell, and while she understood her feelings completely, she also acknowledged the thrill that passed through her at the thought that Kasey cared enough about their almost relationship to feel a surge of jealousy. Lorelei knew that if their roles were reversed, and Kasey was the one heading off across town with the sole intention of flirting with one of her exes, she herself would have turned into the kind of green eyed monster that – while matching the colors in the curtains, walls and pillows that filled the living room – would have eaten itself alive until Kasey had returned to Undersea Cottage and her arms, where she belonged.

Blinking suddenly, Lorelei jumped as the car behind her in traffic laid on the horn. Caught up in a revelation, she had failed to notice that the light had changed from red to green, and she eased off the brake and on the gas pedal, waving an apologetic hand out the window at the other driver, swept away by the realization that she had just admitted to herself that in her arms was where she believed Kasey belonged.

Shivering suddenly, though the late afternoon sun bore down from above and warmed her through the windshield, she allowed herself to think for a moment about the hour she had just spent with Kasey on the sofa, legs intertwined, arms around each other, lips pressed together in gentle, tender caresses that very quickly had turned into heated, urgent movements, raising their temperatures, quickening their heartbeats, demanding connection and consummation.

Breaking apart with racing hearts and heavy breathing, separating with reluctance and an almost painful intensity, they had taken a moment to catch their breath, to find the earth with their feet again, to swim from the deep waters that rushed around them to a place where the waves were no longer crashing over their heads. There was no doubt that the attraction was mutual. Lorelei wanted Kasey. Kasey wanted Lorelei. But Lorelei was bound and determined that their first time together – unclothed and uninhibited – would be slow and deliberate, languid and luxurious, a gentle warmth building to a passionate heat that broke every last barrier between them and set the stage for every other time to follow. A tumble on the sofa was all well and good, and Lorelei had no objection to having many of them with Kasey in the future – loving and laughing together, finding quick heat and swift passion during a stolen hour, throwing the sofa pillows on the floor and making love under the sea – but that was something to dream of, to look forward to in the future, to think about silently in public places, casting secret, covert glances at each other across the table at the coffee house, or over a plate of Jorge's magnificent pastries.

The first time, however, that was going to be different. Lorelei was willing to admit that she was falling in love with Kasey. Willing to accept that she *wanted* to love her, to protect her, to bring a smile to that delicious mouth, light to those depthless dark eyes, to caress her in all the secret places that would make her shiver, make her moan, make her beg for more. More than she had ever known before. More than she might even have imagined. More than Lorelei could give her during a delightful but hurried afternoon quickie on the sofa. And with that admission came the understanding that what she really wanted was to romance Kasey, to captivate her, to coax awake her mermaid heart until she offered it freely, to take her hand and take her heart and sweep her right off her fins. There would be no rushing, no hurry, no swift completion and moving on to other things. Lorelei was determined – she wanted their first time to be perfect.

Jumping again as the voice of the GPS blared to inform her that her destination had been reached, Lorelei winced. Her determination to earn the love of Kasey Martin was unlikely to be aided by her current mission, driving across town to flirt with her ex-girlfriend, but she knew that she was going to do it anyway. She loved Troy also, though in an entirely different and thoroughly platonic way, and he had asked her to do this one little thing, bravely smiling and flirting and teasing, as if his secretly tender heart wasn't broken and long since encapsulated in a small framed photograph, a lifetime of memories, and a candle in a frosted glass holder. For Troy, she would have done almost anything, even travelled to the other end of the Earth to bring him something that he wanted, though his heart's desire would probably turn out to be Italian silk boxer shorts or something equally frivolous. It made no difference – Troy had always, always been there for her. She was going to be there for him. But after this … after this, Kasey.

Leaving Kasey behind in the living room when she went upstairs to touch up her makeup had felt like swimming against a deliberate and stubborn current, but Lorelei had done it. When she returned to the living room, she found Kasey had fallen asleep on the sofa, curled around a satin star fish pillow, her dark head resting on a sea foam green chenille sea horse. Taken aback, Lorelei could not decide if she was most overcome by Kasey's beauty, her innocent vulnerability, or her soft, steady breathing. She had simply drawn the blanket up over Kasey's sleeping shoulder and whispered a wish for sweet dreams, gently kissing the dark, tousled hair that fell across her temple and tumbled over her shoulder.

Shaking her head, Lorelei found herself embarrassingly jealous of a sea foam green chenille sea horse. Tearing herself away from the lovely creature sleeping peacefully on her sofa (well maybe she stared for a *little* while) she had reached for her purse and keys and slipped quietly out the door.

Pulling into a parking space now, after a thirty minute drive filled with thoughts of Kasey, Lorelei drew a deep breath and set her mind on her ex-girlfriend Allison and the task before her. It was time for some strategically enacted tactical flirting. After all, what was good for the Troy was good for the gander ... er, the goose. Gooses. Geese. Whatever! she thought wildly, climbing out of the car and slipping her keys into a pocket (the fabulous flowing skirt had pockets!). All really *was* fair in love and war, and – Lorelei suspected – this might turn out to be both.

Chapter Twenty Three

If Allison Inglis had expected her day to be boring, slow and without surprises, she in no way objected to the vision of turquoise hair and green eyes that appeared quite suddenly in the doorway of her office. In the twelve months since their break up, her ex-girlfriend had clearly found someone or something that made her deliriously happy – Lorelei was radiant.

"Lorelei, you look amazing!" Rising from behind the chrome and glass desk that anchored her elegant office, Allison crossed the thick, modern carpet that tied together the minimalist décor scheme and nearly matched the pale taupe shade of her low but expensive heels.

Catching Lorelei up in a hug, she was surprised to find that she was genuinely happy to see her. Stepping back from the embrace and smiling, she waved her hands in the air, retreating back to the leather armchair behind the desk and shrugging.

"Sorry, Lor, you know I was always a hugger."

Lorelei smiled, not at all discomfited by the embrace but feeling a little bit guilty about her mission. She knew she was there under false pretenses – she wasn't sure she had deserved the friendly greeting, much less the hug. Resolutely she fixed a picture of Troy in her mind (sad Troy, drunk Troy, broken hearted Troy, not fabulous, flamboyant, well dressed and happy Troy) and ordered a stern forward march.

"It's good to see you, Ally," she said, realizing it was true. "Nice place!"

Glancing almost shyly around the elegant chrome and glass of the office, Allison giggled (something she realized she had not done out loud since … well, since Lorelei.) "I know, it's too bare for you – all simplicity and Feng Shui. You'd prefer seashells and bright paintings and silk and sequins."

Lorelei shrugged, wryly aware that Allison was describing Undersea Cottage, even though she had never actually seen it. "I haven't changed," she agreed, crossing the office in a swish of long aquamarine and turquoise skirts and gesturing toward a chair, the thin straps of the white camisole pale against the tan of her shoulders. "Mind if I sit?"

Allison looked flustered. "Of course! I'm sorry!" she cried, "I should have offered. Would you like a drink? I can send for a …"

Lorelei shook her head, unwilling to have Allison go to any trouble and equally unwilling to lie to get what she needed.

"Ally," she said, sinking into the chair amid a settling of graceful fabric and long, slender legs. "I need to ask you for a favor."

Milling around Undersea Cottage in a flurry of needless activity after her unexpected nap, Kasey straightened all the pillows she could usefully straighten, washed the few dishes in the elegant, shell shaped sink, then sat on the ocean colored sofa and stared across the room at the portrait she had drawn of Lorelei.

Attempting to assess it with the critical and trained eye of the artist that she was, she found her sense of perspective skewed, her ability to analyze and recreate muted, her judgement affected by the living, breathing beauty of the subject she had rendered in pencils and charcoal. Drawing Lorelei from memory had been one thing, drawing her from life, a mere fifteen or twenty feet across the back room of the coffee house (before fleeing out the rear exit and panicking behind the dumpster like a ninny) was an enhanced artistic experience, but still a matter of model and artist, proximity and paper.

Now, having come to know Lorelei, to laugh with her, to sit and talk with her, to kiss that willing mouth and hold that graceful hand and feel that lithe body pressed up against hers, it was impossible to look at the portrait – one she knew had already been good before being infused with the actual experience that was Lorelei – without imbuing it with the reality. As she stared, the portrait looked ready to toss its head with a burst of musical laughter, brush hair from its face with a graceful hand, turn brilliant green eyes toward her in the dim, underwater light of the living room, their color slowly darkening with intensity, with expectation, with undeniable desire . . .

Suddenly flustered, Kasey leapt up and began to pace the painted floorboards, determined to slow the flutter of her heart, the spinning of her head, the silly and inexcusable trembling of her hands. She was not a young girl with a crush, stricken silent in the face of the prettiest girl in the school. She was an adult. An actress and an artist. A grown woman with a history and a future, with friends and family and her own heart and mind. Her time with Cassandra had been fraught, their ugly break up had shaken her, made her doubt herself doubt her ability to judge a woman's character, doubt whether she was deserving of the kind of love she read about in the Les Fic novels she indulged in on those long Saturday nights when her date consisted of a pint of ice cream and a bottle of wine. She didn't believe in perfect people. She didn't believe in insta love, she wasn't even certain that she believed in happily ever after – but she did know one thing beyond the shadow of all of those doubts; she believed in Lorelei.

She believed in Lorelei's heart, in her quick wit and her sharp mind, her impossibly adorable smile and her earnest expression, in her love for her friend and in her tender hands, in her intoxicating kisses and her mermaid dreams. Smiling wryly, Kasey sank down on the sofa and shook her head in resigned acceptance of the current state of her heart. Lorelei might not have been actually perfect (though wasn't she, really?) but she was perfect for Kasey. Troy had been right, the smug, well dressed little devil. Kasey had fallen in love with a sea siren, hook line and proverbial sinker, and she knew something else for certain. Lorelei was currently at the office of state records, flirting her heart out with the woman who used to be her girlfriend – and Kasey was sitting in the cottage without her, bereft, forsaken and painfully jealous.

She knew that Lorelei's trip to see – what was her name? Allison? – had been reluctant, hesitant, coerced into action by Troy's Hollywood level charm, baby blue eyes and laser beam dimples. Surely, she thought in haphazard distraction, weapons as potent as his ought to have military applications? If there were such a thing as all gay male battalions, Troy could slay a hundred men at a pop with one of those lazy, seductive smiles he practiced in the mirror. He could probably go so far as to actually bring about world peace. Men in uniform would fall at his feet and the war would be over in a heartbeat.

Sighing, Kasey wondered what it felt like to have that kind of effect on the people one wanted to impress, to attract, even to seduce. She wished she had a tenth of Troy's swagger, his suave moves and innocent countenance, and she certainly would not have said no to an offer of those dimples. Even she, who had not had interest in a boy since that one disastrous high school dance (and even that was forced and fake and what she thought she was "supposed" to feel) could not resist Troy when he was intent on conniving her, and this time he had connived her right into falling for Lorelei. Not that it had been difficult.

Smiling suddenly, she hid her face in the curves of a fringed velvet pillow that might have been a jellyfish, blushing like a twelve year old girl. The pillow, scented with the essential oils Lorelei wore as perfume, was soft and sweet, and Kasey smiled again at the thought of it coming in contact with Lorelei's skin. For a moment she, too, found herself possessing the ridiculous ability to be jealous of a throw pillow.

Deeply inhaling the scent of blended lavender, bergamot, and rosemary that made it seem as if Lorelei were there in the room beside her, she shook her head, unable to hold a grudge against Troy, against Lorelei, against the velvet pillow, or even against Allison whatever-her-name-was. She might not have had the triple threat powers of sass, sweetness and seduction that Troy wielded with natural born ease and practiced diligence, but Lorelei looked at her and made her feel as if she did. Kasey had met someone wonderful, whispered and laughed with her, kissed her and trusted her with the carefully taped together pieces of her formerly broken heart. She knew she was already far happier than she had ever been before.

Chapter Twenty Four

When Lorelei returned late that afternoon, she smelled of designer perfume, triple lattes, information and success. The perfume, restricted to one shoulder and the result of no more than a 'no hard feelings, we're still friends, aren't we?' hug from Allison the ex, faded quickly as the lavender, bergamot and rosemary of Undersea Cottage drew her into its embrace, and she curled on the sofa with Kasey, a Starbucks cup in each hand and a bakery bag from a local patisserie on the cushion between them. The pastries it contained were not a match for the baked divinity Jorge created out of thin air, flour and enchantment, but – as Kasey realized that she had more or less forgotten to eat anything all day – they sure as hell hit the spot.

Speaking of hitting the spot, she thought hazily, as Lorelei's lips explored the sensitive place just beneath her ear, Lorelei did seem to have an unerring sense of direction. She was – as Kasey was coming to expect – a exquisite combination of enticing, sexy, sweet and sensual; the perfect balance of inciting desire and waiting for consent. Kasey shivered. Despite the impracticality of spending the rest of her life in an underwater living room with a turquoise haired mermaid who tasted of new beginnings, she knew that there were other considerations important to the both of them, however tempted they were to set them aside and simply melt into each other instead.

Troy needed them, and he, who had always been there for each of them no matter what the circumstances, had endured the painful extremity of asking. Fiercely proud, thoroughly independent, surviving his losses by means of cherished memories and sheer determination, Troy had come to them for help despite his penchant for fighting his battles in solitude. Lonely, heartbreaking, well dressed solitude. Both Lorelei and Kasey understood what that had cost him.

Sitting up against the cushions despite the protests coming in from all points of her body (some points more vociferously than others) Kasey shook her head to clear it of caresses and kisses, setting a small mountain of throw pillows between them on the sofa, like an ocean themed barricade from the French revolution.

"Troy," she said, breathless and blushing, holding out both hands toward Lorelei as if to push her away. Or draw her closer. The jury was still out on that one – in fact Kasey suspected they had recessed entirely and would not return to the courtroom until after the weekend. And while the jury was sequestered, she and Lorelei might as well…

"Troy!" Lorelei echoed, even guilt sitting pretty on her features. "Oh my god, how could I have forgotten!"

Her eyes, deep, sparkling green and not in the habit of telling her lies, answered the question for her. Sitting on the other end of sofa, behind a haphazardly constructed pillow fort of oceanic elements in silk and brocade and velvet, sat the woman who could drive even the most simple and basic of thoughts from her head without so much as batting one of those long eyelashes against the smooth olive skin above her cheekbone. Intrigue and sleuthing? Questions and answers? Mystery and secrets? Lorelei was lucky if – in the presence of Kasey Martin – she remembered how to breathe.

"Troy," Kasey reminded her breathlessly, scooching a little farther away on the sofa, even as she leaned forward to be closer to Lorelei as if drawn by a magnetism she did not understand. Perhaps the same magnetism that drew the waves to shore and let them go, as the tides reacted to the siren song of the moon.

"Troy," Lorelei confirmed, hastily building a pillow fort of her own. "I went to the Indiana hall of records to ask questions for Troy."

The statement was a simple reassertion of facts that both of them already knew, and Kasey curled her fingers around Lorelei's and sat up on the cushions.

"Tell me," she said breathlessly, banishing thoughts of soft lips and scented skin to a corner of her mind she well knew she would revisit later. "What did you find out?"

Equally determined to focus on the task at hand, Lorelei settled behind the barricade of throw pillows and told her.

Allison Inglis, intrigued and more than willing to help, had agreed that the situation Troy had described sounded suspicious. Accessing information that neither Troy nor Lorelei would have been able to, her smooth forehead had furrowed, her pretty eyes narrowed, and she had tapped a sleek Waterford pen against the chrome and glass of her expensive desk top with a tempo that increased with each screen she opened on her slender silver laptop.

According to Allison's sources, and Lorelei trusted her utterly, a set of papers had been filed listing the property, the theatre, and all its contents as having been purchased nearly three years earlier. The papers, and the official listing in the database, were nowhere to be found, and all traces of the transaction had been erased from the official records. Finding evidence of the sale—a small notation in a weekly report recorded by a diligent secretary–took nearly an hour of digging, but by the time she found it, Allison had become determined to research the mystery to its conclusion. She did not like irregularities, did not like questionable records, had always had a fondness for Troy, and would do anything for Lorelei.

Smiling deeply, her thanks fervent and genuine, Lorelei had returned to Undersea Cottage, her head buzzing with thoughts and conjecture, thankful that her breakup with Allison Inglis had ended amiably and with mutual fondness. She felt as if she had reconnected with an old friend, found a staunch and formidable ally, and helped Troy at the same time.

Chapter Twenty Five

If Lorelei's afternoon with Allison Inglis had been a qualified success, Troy's morning excursion (about which he had been determinedly and suspiciously vague) had netted him exactly nothing – or at least, nothing useful.

"I tried to get information from the man guarding the door to the inner sanctum," he said, referring to the offices of the law firm with a mixture of disgust and scathing sarcasm. "I hit a brick wall. A brick wall with silk ivy, recessed lighting and expensive reproduction prints from the museum of modern art."

He flopped down on the sea foam green sofa in the middle of Lorelei's living room, realized he was being untidy, and sat up, swiping in frustration at a casual and careless hair style on which he had spent an hour and several over priced hair products. Other people used hair spray, gel, mousse, pomade – Troy (as he repeated frequently and with rapidly depleting patience) used *Hair Product*. He used capital letters every time he said it.

"Was the lawyer uncooperative?" Lorelei handed him a bottle of San Pellegrino (she always kept some on hand in case he dropped by unannounced, which was rarely. Troy liked to be announced.)

"If by uncooperative you mean straight, then yes, he was uncooperative," Troy said glumly. He raised a frustrated eyebrow. "The woman partner was in the other office," he shook his head. "But I didn't get anywhere with her either. I'm doomed."

Kasey patted his shoulder, shocked to hear that the inimitable Troy Preston charm (patent pending) had struck out twice in one day. It was unheard of.

"Lesbian?" Lorelei ventured, equally aware of his usual success rate. Charm was a precision instrument, and Troy was a virtuoso.

Troy reached for a chenille and silk sea anemone and placed it deliberately over his face, bending his arms to hold it in place and locking his elbows dramatically. "Dooooomed..." he declaimed from beneath it.

Kasey's brow furrowed in concentration as a thought vibrated quietly in the back of her head, teasing her with the illusion of great importance without revealing why. Closing her eyes, she focused on the thought, coaxing it forward, grasping at it while it flashed by like quicksilver without stopping. A moment later, she finally recognized what the thought had been trying to tell her.

"Troy," she said, so quietly that Lorelei and Troy nearly didn't hear her. "What was the name of the law firm you went to?" Her voice was suddenly taut, her throat tight, her expression wary and guarded.

Emerging from underneath the pillow without a hair out of place, Troy narrowed his eyes. "Darling," he demanded, "please tell me that you think you might be on to something?"

Lorelei sidled closer to Kasey, slipping an arm around the curve of her waist. "Kasey? Kasey, what is it?"

Kasey shook her head, hoping against hope that she was wrong, that it was nothing, that there were a dozen law firms in the city of Bloomington whose partners included a Troy-resistant male attorney and a lesbian lawyer.

Troy fished a business card out of the inner pocket concealed in the silk lining of his suit jacket, handing it to Kasey with a pained expression. "Viper, Jackal and Weasel," he said with a shake of his head, as Kasey's eyes scanned the gold embossed business card and widened. "Otherwise known as Monteforte, Price, and Riskin."

Lorelei gasped. "Troy!" she cried, spinning on the sofa cushion to face him, her expression horrified. "You went to *their* office? After that woman threatened you? Are you crazy?"

Troy shrugged. "Crazy like a fox," he protested, "not that it did any good. I thought I could maybe get in with one of the other partners, find out what they're trying to hide." His expression darkened. "Because they are hiding something, darling, they *are*."

"I know they are!" Lorelei cried, unable to keep herself from seizing his hand and holding on to him as though she could keep him from running off into untenable situations. Especially without backup. "Did you think they were going to just tell you whatever you wanted to know?"

Troy just flashed his dimples momentarily, indicating with a sly wink that he had. "I sent that viper woman flowers after she threw me out of the office," he said with a stubborn resurgence of his old sparkle, squeezing the fingers that Lorelei had wrapped around his hand. "It seemed only polite since she sent me a present first." That was Troy – like a beach ball held underwater, only to surge upward and burst free the moment whoever was holding it under let go.

Lorelei tipped her turquoise head suspiciously. "A present?"

Troy nodded brightly back at her, a fierce and false optimism undergirding his answer. "My first legal trespass warning!" he said cheerfully, reminding them without a trace of modesty that he was always dressed for a photographic opportunity. "At least my mug shot will be fabulous after I …"

"Troy!" Lorelei meant business. "You'd better not! Don't you go anywhere near that office again!"

Troy pretended to pout. "I think I can legally go within five hundred feet of the building. Can't I at least set the trespass warning on fire and leave in on their doorstep? I can probably throw it from five hundred feet away if I make it into a paper airplane first." He reached and tucked Kasey's hand beneath his elbow. "My eyes look really good by firelight," he whispered, knowing that he was in trouble with Lorelei and aligning himself with his remaining ally.

Tender hearted and trusting, Kasey would usually have gone along with anything he said, but her set expression and tight lips made it clear that she had more worrying things on her mind than Troy deliberately violating a trespass warning. Lorelei's scolding expression became one of concern.

"Kasey?"

"That woman," Kasey said quietly, amazed to hear her voice actually leaving her lips and rising into the air between them. "Reid what's her name, the lawyer from the theatre…"

Lorelei pushed Troy out of the way, taking Kasey's hand from him and ignoring his good natured grumbling. "What about her?"

Kasey drew a deep a shuddering breath, all of her old fears, her old insecurities, every cruel thing Cassandra had said to her the day she found out about the affair rising up as if to drown her. All the warmth, the sense of well being, of being cherished, of being protected that she had felt with Lorelei suddenly seemed like a beautiful dream that she had lived at night, only to wake up and discover it was not real.

"I met her at the corporate banquet the night we were mermaids," she said quietly, fixing her wide and anxious eyes on Lorelei for courage. "She's dating my ex-girlfriend. Maybe I could…"

Sitting up, Troy seized her hand again, all traces of affable teasing suddenly vanished. "No, darling," he protested, his expression suddenly determined. "You don't go anywhere near that horrible woman. I won't have it."

His expression was fierce and set, impossible to misinterpret, just as he intended for it to be. Sending spunky, feisty Lorelei to chat up an affable old flame long after an amiable and mutual breakup was one thing. Exposing sweet, vulnerable Kasey to the teeth of a shark in Chanel was another. It was not to be countenanced.

Sighing, Troy shook his head again, mistakenly assuming that Kasey would dutifully agree to his opinion. He wanted to protect her, had always been there to protect her, since the day they had become friends. It did not occur to him that in Kasey, there was a new flame burning, a new strength growing, increasing, filling up the spaces that had been hollowed out by betrayal and lies and cheating women who didn't care who they hurt but should have. Kasey did not protest out loud, did not tell him that she loved him but was going to do whatever she decided to do regardless of what he told her. She did not argue with him. She did not share her intentions. She did not explain that even the short time she had spent with Lorelei (was she "with" Lorelei? Kasey wondered breathlessly, was that what this was?) had changed her whole outlook, her whole demeanor, giving rise to strength and confidence that wavered in the face of talking to Reid Monteforte, or Cassandra Carat, but did not crumble. Kasey did not articulate any of these things – especially not to Troy - but she held them in her heart, examined them in secret surprise, and knew them to be true.

Beside her on the sofa, Troy, too, was lost in thought, his expression weary for a moment but filled with determination. He wished he could buy the theatre outright and keep it safe in perpetuity from wrecking balls and progress and she-devils in designer stilettos. He wished he had the courage and dignity that Matteo had shown in the face of terminal illness. He wished he could wrap that bravery around himself like the slim leather Tom Ford belt that circled his waist, or better yet wrap Matteo's arms around him where they belonged, instead of forcing himself to remember that those arms would never wrap around him again. He wished he had more time. More time to tell Matteo he would love him forever, more time to raise the money to save Matteo's theatre, more time to think of a way to stop Reid Monteforte and her clients from turning Matteo's last masterpiece into dust and splinters and ashes. He wished he had more time.

Captivated, Lorelei stared at Troy and Kasey for a moment, feeling a surge of emotion in her chest at the thought of these two people – one long since loved and adored, and the other newly so – who meant so much in her life that words were inadequate to describe how strong, how true, how deep the feelings went. She had loved Troy through ten years of friendship and adventure and considered him an older brother (a well-dressed, fabulous, meddling, bossy older brother) – there was nothing she would not do for him, or he for her.

She also did not shy away from associating the word love with thoughts of Kasey Martin. She was confident, unafraid, certain that love was exactly what she was feeling despite the fact that it was new and young and just beginning. Unlike her love for Troy, however, she knew that her love for Kasey was different. It was saturating, encompassing, heated and growing, a hot ember of emotion and desire that could either bring warmth and light and comfort, or heat and fire and glory. Deliberately, she forced herself to focus on the two people sitting with her on the sofa, as if memorizing their faces, their posture, the sound of their breathing, knowing in her heart that in the absence of close knit family members of her own, they had become her family.

Troy and Kasey looked like twin actors on a movie set, deep in thought while cameras rolled, each experiencing introspective inner monologues about to be filmed as a montage with music playing over them. Unable to bear their melancholy, Lorelei shattered the illusion. "What are you going to do?" she asked Troy.

Turning to her, Troy shook his head slightly, as if banishing the specter of doubt and indecision to some distant hell where there were no cappuccinos or designer neckties, or fashion weeks in Paris. His expression had turned mildly dangerous and decidedly cagey.

"Whatever it takes," he answered grimly.

Chapter Twenty Six

When Troy left Undersea Cottage a short time later, it was with a controlled mix of anxiety, determination, and despair. Entering the beautifully decorated confines of his condo upon returning, he dropped his keys in the crystal bowl on the little marble topped table near the entrance and stood for a moment in the center of the elegant carpet, listening to the sound of his heartbeat in the quiet, his mind in the center of the condo with him, but his heart in a place he had left two years before. In that place, Matteo Fabiano was alive and well, his dark eyes filled with love and laughter, his expression becoming avid when he engaged in creative pursuits, becoming tender when he looked at Troy, becoming heated when Troy looked back at him. The memories ended, as they always did, in a cold, white hospital room, surrounded not by roses and symphonies and paintings and sculpture, but by tubes and wires and beeping monitors. Troy hated that part of the memories, but cherished it also, because those tragic moments with Matteo had been his last. Remembering the end was the price he paid for remembering all the wonderful memories that came before. Of course, the ending was always the same, like a sad movie that tore his heart out just before the final credits. Matteo had closed his eyes at the very end, his fingers wrapped tightly around Troy's hand, leaving behind pain and sickness and finally life itself, but still holding on to Troy. Troy had never let go either.

Shaking his head to clear it, Troy turned toward the bedroom, the leather of his shoes making no sound on the thick pile of the carpet. Sliding open the top drawer of his dresser, the wood sliding smoothly along the metal tracks, he drew out a carved wooden box, closing the drawer with his precisely ironed elbow and turning to sit on the bed. Drawing a deep breath and holding it for a moment, he steeled himself for the exquisite pain of remembering all that he had once had, and all that he had lost.

When he had been alive, before illness had overtaken him, before medication had dulled his senses, before hospitals had pulled him from the bed and side of the man that he loved, Matteo had been a conscientious and sensitive lover. He sent roses, he appeared with takeout lunches in unexpected places, he cooked candlelit dinners for two and left trails of rose petals leading to the bedroom. And every week, without fail for as long as he could, he wrote love letters. Romantic letters, beautiful letters, prose and poetry, declarations of forever, a baring of his soul and heart that he never shared with anybody else.

Troy had kept every one of those letters, treasured them, wept over them when no one was watching, read them again and again until their corners were worn, their ink faded, their memories as poignant as ever. Some days he read every single letter – every single letter except for one. The last letter, the final letter, had been sent through the mail, as Matteo's letters sometimes were. Though usually more inclined to tuck the letters into bouquets of hothouse flowers, leave them on Troy's pillow as he slept or to be found beside his morning coffee when he woke, Matteo occasionally put them into an envelope, addressed them to the same condo in which he lived, put a stamp on them and dropped them into the mailbox that stood on the corner of their street. He had been old fashioned and appreciative of traditional arts like letter writing and fountain pens, original poetry and sealing wax, and he always said he liked the idea of Troy rifling through a handful of bills and junk mail and advertising circulars and coming across a pale crème envelope bearing his name, the faint scent of his lover's cologne and professions of undying love.

Drawing a deep breath to ease the tightness in his chest, Troy drew that final letter from the bottom of the wooden box, knowing without raising it to his nose that the faint, barely there scent of cologne was almost gone entirely. Matteo had professed undying love, and – Troy knew with his whole heart – that love had never died. But Matteo had. Sliding his thumb gently across the smooth surface of the still sealed thick vellum envelope, he set the letter carefully back in the secret, cherished box, stacking the other letters neatly atop it, and closing Matteo's scent, his words, his memory, inside the box once again.

He had not read that final letter, was not certain he would ever read it, knowing that once he did that there would never be another. Reading that final letter was to admit that Matteo was really and truly never coming back, and that he would never again speak or write or act out of love. Troy wasn't ready to face that, and he knew it.

Rising, he crossed the room and pushed through the door, swiping the moisture from the blue of his eyes and striding toward the desk in his study. There, a sleek, streamlined laptop blinked into life at the touch of a button, its desktop wallpaper a photograph of one of Matteo's beautiful paintings. Troy had considered using a picture of Matteo for the wallpaper but hadn't – he knew all too well that there was already a knife in his heart; he didn't need to twist it. Matteo would have understood.

Desperate and without much hope, Troy logged into his online banking app and spent hours crunching numbers, moving assets, applying for loans he could never repay, and that would never come through before morning, when the theatre would go on the auction block and be purchased by the cutthroat lawyers for their corporate clients and destroyed. Once again, he needed more time. Grimly, he logged onto the auction site at midnight, waited for the online bid application to open, and made a bid to buy the theatre with money he knew he did not possess. The gesture was useless, pointless, absolutely hopeless, but he did it anyway.

Chapter Twenty Seven

If Cassandra Carat had been under the impression that cheating on Kasey to be with Reid Monteforte was in any way a relationship upgrade, she discovered fairly quickly that it was not. Reid was beautiful, there was no denying the fact – polished and expensive and flawless on the surface – but her interest in Cassandra had from the beginning had more to do with manipulation and power, with proving to yet another sweet innocent somebody that the love of her life could be turned and taken, and with seeing something pretty and buying it outright even though it should not have been for sale.

Turning Cassandra's head with designer clothes and fancy cars, hothouse roses and diamond earrings had been simple, and Reid had taken Kasey's girlfriend to bed with no regrets whatsoever and both taken and demanded whatever she wanted. Cassandra had given both, willingly. If Reid had given a thought at all to the woman Cassandra was cheating on, to the relationship she had shattered by bedding Cassandra (frequently and thoroughly) to the innocence she had broken by methodically ordering Cassandra to throw Kasey to the curb, she would have felt no more regret than she would have felt in stepping on an ant.

Reid liked things that were bright and shiny, she liked having her way with them, and she liked to possess them – at least until they began to bore her. That she would eventually also cheat on Cassandra was merely a matter of whim and opportunity, and when the time came, she would not hesitate to cast Cassandra away just as Cassandra had cast away Kasey. Cassandra didn't know any of this yet, of course, awash in the money and high society whirlwind through which Reid was currently escorting her, but Karma knew. And Karma was riding a fast train in Cassandra's direction.

The day of the sale, when Matteo Fabiano's theatre and Troy Preston's heart were put on the auction block side by side, Reid had brought Cassandra to the office with her, showing off her latest acquisition as she would an elegant pair of shoes or a new car. Her audience, of course, was curated and limited, comprised of a bevy of receptionists, clerks and under secretaries. Cassandra, after all, might have been a Jaguar or a BMW, but she wasn't a Lamborghini. She was useful, though, Reid thought with absolutely no emotional attachment, as she slid a shapely, stockinged foot out of one sleek black pump and rested it on Cassandra's shoulder, her eyes cold as she stared up at the ceiling.

Beneath her massive mahogany executive desk, currently on her knees and hidden from sight, Cassandra Carat was performing the function for which Reid had brought her to the office. In Cassandra's imagination, the clandestine assignation Reid had suggested had seemed daring and romantic, a hint of sexual scandal in an office building filled with wealthy, powerful people, but in reality it was cramped, uncomfortable, and a hairsbreadth from being humiliating. It was not that Cassandra had any objections to finding herself ensconced between the salon tanned and gym toned thighs of the beautiful Reid Monteforte – it was that Reid had neither closed her office door nor put her calls on hold to enjoy it.

Sitting back on her heels at a peremptory shove from the woman in the executive leather desk chair above her, Cassandra blinked suddenly, pushing her disheveled hair away from her forehead and crouching on the carpet, feeling more than a little bit foolish.

"I don't care if he did place a bid on the building!" Reid was snarling into an appallingly expensive cell phone. "He will not be allowed to stop us from acquiring that property. I want this finished, do you hear me?"

Raising a carefully shaped and shaded eyebrow, Cassandra listened unabashedly, a rush of cool air from the climate control vent cooling her cheeks as Reid rose from the chair, returning her foot to her shoe in one smooth motion as she rose to stalk around the office.

"Well they only have to honor the bid if it remains on the table," she snapped, every hair in place as she moved to stand at the floor to ceiling window, the slick black sheen of her shoes sinking into the thick carpeting that covered the office. "We just have to convince the pestilential little nobody to withdraw his offer."

A silence settled over the office as a disembodied voice, echoing faintly from the cell phone, posed a prolonged series of questions that made Reid's sculpted lips curl against her perfect teeth: a feral super model smile thirsty for the throat of its prey. Cautiously, Cassandra emerged from under the desk.

"He simply needs to be shown that his interference will not be tolerated," Reid snapped suddenly, disconnecting the call and hurling the cell phone into the elegant throw pillows that guarded both ends of a fine leather sofa, symmetrical and expensive but artistically uninspired. "Leave him to me."

Her last words, spoken for the benefit of her own ears alone, caused goosebumps to rise on Cassandra's arms, but any questions or concerns Kasey's ex-girlfriend might have voiced were suddenly crushed beneath a pair of hard lips, ruby red and unyielding, aroused by the thought of destroying an enemy. A shiny black stiletto finally kicked shut the door. The encounter that followed – heated and demanding – drove any thoughts whatsoever from Cassandra's mind.

After, somehow still pristine and perfect, Reid rose from the sleek leather of the sofa with long legged grace and casual surety, dropping three one hundred dollar bills on the bare skin of Cassandra's breast, still flushed from exertion and desire.

"Go buy yourself a present, Pussycat," she said dismissively, reaching for the cell phone that had tumbled from the cushions to the carpet. "I have work to do."

Chapter Twenty Eight

Rising from the sheets of his empty bed the following morning weary and without hope regarding the theatre, Troy carefully laid out an elegant blue suit, carefully tailored and freshly dry cleaned, and coupled it with a pristine white shirt and silk tie. He did not place much confidence in the chance that he could convince a group of prospective investors into saving the theatre as easily as he had railroaded Lorelei into buying Undersea Cottage, but he intended to place his faith in dimples and Dior and try it anyway.

Dressing methodically, he made his way to the kitchen in stocking feet, reaching for a thickly quilted paper towel to buff an almost nonexistent smudge from the surface of the shoe he was carrying. Preoccupied and dull with sorrow, he never even saw the three men hovering in his foyer until they had already seized him, and he watched the polished shoe fall from his hand to the carpet in utter confusion, his ears ringing as a meaty fist dealt him a blow to the temple that drove him to his knees. The next strike was no kinder, and was followed by another, and another, two sets of hands holding his elbows in a bruising grip while the third man dealt out violence with the casual ease of a well paid enforcer. When Troy finally lost consciousness, minutes or hours later, the leather of the shoe, his fine white shirt, and the pale pattern of the carpet were spattered with bright, wet splashes of red.

In the ascetically bare and painfully elegant high rise office building that Reid Monteforte shared with her partners, the man standing in front of the mahogany desk looked as out of place as a lumberjack in Buckingham palace. Curling her lip, Reid tossed him an antibacterial wipe in a sealed package, shaking her head as he caught it in one huge fist.

"Wash that blood off your hands," she snapped, not at all discomfited by the fact that the dried smears of red on the scowling man's knuckles might as well have been on her own. "Can't you at least attempt to be discreet?"

She dropped a thick envelope filled with unmarked bills on the top of the desk in sneering refusal to so much as accidentally brush his fingertips with hers by handing it to him. "Has our little activist been convinced that now is not a healthy time to patronize the arts?"

The man rolled his eyes at her, appreciative of the lucrative payment, but far less impressed by Reid than she intended him to be.

"If you mean did he decide to withdraw his bid on the theatre building," he said, slipping the envelope into his pocket, "you'll have to ask him when he wakes up." His cruel chuckle faded to be replaced by an expression of labored concentration as he began trying to work out how to cheat his partners of their share of the money. After all, he had done all the work. All they had done was hold Troy Preston still while he beat him.

Reid shook her head sharply, elegant gold and diamond earrings glinting at her ear lobes. "You'd better not have killed him," she muttered, unwilling to countenance the complications that would engender.

"Why not?" the thug grumbled, turning away and heading toward the doorway with his money. "Wouldn't that solve the problem just as easily?"

As the door closed behind him, Reid sank into her leather chair and drew the flat blade of a brass and mother-of-pearl letter opener across the pad of her finger, musing that the man was probably right. Of course, if – or more likely when – she dealt permanently with the problem of Troy Preston, she wouldn't be stupid enough to leave behind witnesses or evidence or a body for the police to investigate. She curled her lip again. And she certainly wouldn't leave blood to be found beneath her fingernails.

Leaning back against the sleek leather of the chair, she lazily regretting sending Cassandra out shopping again that morning to get rid of her. Contemplating the complete and utter destruction of someone who was in her way always made her hot, and she could have put Cassandra to good use underneath the desk. Shaking her head, Reid shrugged.

Troy Preston was definitely in her way. He would either take the hint and back off, or she would have to take more permanent measures. She wasn't about to let anyone find out the illegal lengths she had gone to in order to procure the property that housed the theatre, or that her supposed clients – fabricated and nonexistent – had nothing whatsoever to do with her determination to purchase the property. That slick little caterer was far more clever than she had given him credit for, and had stumbled into a position that could ruin her completely if he ever figured out what he was sitting on. Her intention all along had been to acquire and then sell that property for a fortune, and when opportunity had presented itself, she had stolen papers, forged documents and erased legal records to clear the way.

The deception, one of her earliest and least sophisticated criminal enterprises, had been amateurish and sloppy. She would have pretended it had never happened and abandoned the scheme entirely if those damned preservationists had not brought about renewed interest in the theatre and that interfering caterer had not decided to be Joan of Arc in a Balenciaga button down. Now she was backed into a corner.

If she could purchase the property outright, in the name of a shell corporation, she could prevent anyone from digging too deeply into the series of irregularities that had supposedly derailed its previous sale. Reid, who had herself derailed the previous sale, could sit on the property until the buzz died down, then resell it at a huge profit. She would, of course, bulldoze the building right away out of spite. With the money from the eventual sale she intended to buy out her partners, elevate her own position, and become wildly successful and filthy rich. Distractedly, she made a note to trade Cassandra in for a newer, more expensive model, and soon. Reid Monteforte was going places, and she didn't care who she destroyed on her way.

Chapter Twenty Nine

While the sunlight outside of Undersea Cottage spilled down in shades of gold from a clear blue sky, inside Lorelei's living room the light was muted, ethereal and soft, screened through pale-tinted stained glass and sheer green and blue curtains, just at Matteo Fabiano had intended. Walking barefoot from the kitchen, soft cotton skirts brushing her calves and ankles, Lorelei set an etched glass tray on the coffee table and smiled. The contents of the tray, turkey sandwiches, glasses of sweet-tart lemonade and white ceramic bowls of fresh leaf salad, were simple and everyday, a commonplace, familiar offering from one friend to another, the same sort of lunch shared a thousand times over in a thousand living rooms between thousands of people in thousands of towns over, every single day. It was nothing out of the ordinary, nothing spectacular, and yet in that moment, as a heartfelt offering from one soul to another, it might as well have been diamonds from Cartier, jewelry from Tiffany's, or gold, frankincense and myrrh.

Overcome with emotions she could not put into words yet compelled in the heart of the moment to try, Kasey stared for a moment at the plate Lorelei had handed her, feeling as if something as simple as a sandwich and salad were a strange and anachronistic element in a day that felt – indescribably and inexplicably — utterly extraordinary.

Lowering her eyebrows, soft graceful curves as shapely as the rest of her, Lorelei tipped her head sideways, a sleek cascade of turquoise strands sliding across her cheek at the motion.

"Is something wrong?" she asked, trying and failing to interpret the expression Kasey was wearing. "Are you one of those people who likes the crust cut off their sandwiches? Because I can do that if you want me to. I used to be one of those people. I don't know why, but for years I wouldn't touch a sandwich with the crust still on it," she admitted, sinking onto the sofa. "I had no logical reason for a deep seated suspicion of fresh baked bread crust, you understand, but I swore an oath and I kept it. You too?"

Letting a quiet breath out between soft lips that Lorelei had already decided on for dessert, Kasey shook her head, tangled up in thoughts and emotions and fears and hopes and worries about a thousand things that would probably never happen, and one thing that might.

"Look," she said hesitantly, certain of nothing except that if she blew a chance at a real relationship with this woman by saying something stupid, she would never forgive herself. "Can we talk?"

At her words, Lorelei's face fell, and she set her lunch plate down with a faint clatter on the edge of the coffee table. "Have I done something wrong?" she said quietly, her easy, breezy confidence faltering as if the wind that filled her sails had suddenly fallen silent. "Whatever I did, I'm sorry."

Wide eyed, Kasey set her plate down beside Lorelei's, stunned by the thought that this gorgeous, confident creature had no idea that she was, essentially, perfect. "Oh no!" she heard herself saying, her voice rising in the cool hush of the living room as though it belonged to someone else entirely. "It isn't you, it's me."

Lorelei's chest tightened with the certain knowledge that she cared a great deal more about what Kasey Martin thought of her than she had previously admitted. "Those words are usually the kiss of death for a relationship," she murmured.

Horrified, Kasey waved her hands in the air as if she could gather the words she had spoken and put them back where they came from.

"Oh no!" she said again, knowing she was repeating herself, knowing she was making it worse, knowing she was being maddeningly confusing but too flustered to fix it. "It isn't like that, not at all! It's just that..." her whirling thoughts stopped suddenly, finding a tiny, unexpected haven in the storm and determinedly dropping anchor. "Did you say relationship?"

Lorelei smiled hesitantly. "I did," she admitted, her words cautious, gentle, calculated to reassure Kasey's doubts, not cause them to stampede out the door of the cottage. "Are you...does that make you uncomfortable?"

Wide eyed, stunned for moment, Kasey shook her head wordlessly, reaching across two plates of salad and untrimmed breadcrusts to take Lorelei's hand. The gesture was instinctual, without thought, and her fingers trembled faintly.

"N-no, not at all," she breathed, suddenly acutely aware of the sofa cushions underneath her, the woven throw rug beneath her bare feet, the softness of

Lorelei's hand in hers, the faint scent of fresh bread and olive oil vinaigrette: all the tiny minutiae that made up this single, unexpected moment that she was suddenly willing to admit that she had hoped for. Taking a deep breath, she met the green eyes that regarded her carefully from only a few feet away, swallowing her doubts and hesitation and realizing that she would rather drown in possibility than stay safe on dry land without Lorelei. Suddenly those stupid obscure sea siren folk songs made all kinds of sense.

"That's what I wanted to talk to you about," she said softly, feeling a thrill course through her at the idea that she was speaking her mind, her heart, recognizing what it was that she wanted and reaching out in the hope that it could be hers. "I…" she took a deep breath and finished the sentence in a rush. "I've never felt like this about anyone before." She felt her cheeks darkening with a blush she had no idea was both adorable and sexy. "I'm so happy when I'm with you," she went on, taking courage from the tender warmth that now filled Lorelei's expression and the gentle pressure from Lorelei's fingers on the back of her hand. "I feel like anything is possible, like I am capable and— and beautiful and smart and desirable, and I love feeling like that. It's…not something that I'm used to." She fell silent, unsure whether she sounded narcissistic or selfish, and worried that she sounded like both.

"That's because you are all of those things," Lorelei said quietly, leaning closer to her across the sofa cushions. "Of course you are." Her voice softened in surprise. "Don't you know that?"

Kasey drew another breath, shaking her head faintly at the realization that if she did not remind herself to breathe, she would pass out, and that there was nothing romantic about a trip to the emergency room. The truth was that she did not possess—had never possessed—the kind of confidence that made her believe she was worthy to be loved by someone like Lorelei, but that being with Lorelei had begun to *give* her that confidence, and with it the desire for something more, something real, something that would last longer than a night, a week, a month, longer than a short term relationship or even a couple of years before it faded, crumbled and became something else entirely.

Quietly, Lorelei waited, tender and respectful, wondering if Kasey had any idea how beautiful she looked right that moment, sun and light casting competing shadows across her face as if she were a canvas and the world needed for her likeness to be captured, preserved for future generations who doubted that any one woman could at the same time be so sweet and good and loving and loyal. Catching her own breath, Lorelei—no stranger to relationships and breakups and new beginnings—realized with a sense of absolute certainty that if Kasey Martin was not the actual origin of every love song, every romantic movie, every sappy valentine's day card and every bouquet of perfect roses, well then, she ought to be.

"I think I'm falling in love with you," Kasey said suddenly, breathlessly, her hand still tight in Lorelei's. "And I know that makes no sense because I barely know you and we've only just met, but…" her eyelashes, coal black and curving, swept down against the dusky skin beneath her eyes. "I needed for you to know."

For a moment Lorelei was silent, aware of her heart beating as if it had just resumed the rhythm that had paused while Kasey struggled to speak those words.

Suddenly she smiled. Those words! A sudden sense of unexpected joy rushed through her like a flood, sweeping away every doubt, every hesitation, every moment of wondering whether Kasey might ever reciprocate the feelings she, too, had been keeping inside her heart, celebrated but silent.

"I'm falling in love with you, too," she said at last, reaching across the space between them to take Kasey's other hand in hers. "I wanted to tell you, but I was worried you weren't ready to hear it." She smiled gently. "I want you to know that, but whatever else you still need to say, I am here to listen."

Kasey smiled a shaky smile, as relieved as if she had just crossed a slender tightrope over a pit of alligators and arrived safely in Lorelei's arms on the other side of a bottomless chasm.

"No, I'm good now," she murmured softly. "Though I did have charts and research and a power point presentation prepared." Her smile quirked up on one side as relief gave way to joy. "But I'll need an extension cord."

Lorelei leaned across the space between them and kissed her softly, Kasey's hands still wrapped up in hers. "Will you settle for two hundred kisses and sandwiches with the crust on?"

Kasey smiled and felt herself falling into Lorelei's eyes, just like all those stupid romance novels she had always scorned. Sighing happily, she decided she might have to rethink her literary prejudices. "That sounds perfect," she whispered, and returned the first of the next two hundred kisses.

Chapter Thirty

Despite the admitted allure of turkey sandwiches and homemade olive oil vinaigrette, Kasey and Lorelei soon forgot all about lunch and abandoned the living room for the soft swish of ocean sounds and the silky welcome of the sheets on Lorelei's bed, the undersea atmosphere created by texture, sound and color only adding to the enchantment of the encounter.

Almost breathless in the moment, and at the same time drinking in Lorelei like the air that sustained her, Kasey reveled in the intimate and sensual connection she felt with this woman who had captivated her, body, heart, and spirit. Immersed fully in the act of exploration, of experience and discovery, her graceful artist's fingers curled around soft curves and against smooth skin as if discovering a brand new masterpiece. In a way, she almost was.

Her heart thudding an echo in rhythmic celebration, Lorelei held Kasey tenderly, carefully, as though she were as precious as a jewel and fragile as a seashell—some new and exotic strain of coral that might break if handled roughly, her heart the luminescent pearl at the center of an oyster. The ocean sounds that whispered through the hidden speakers embedded in the walls of the bedroom seemed to attune to their speeding heartbeats, rushing and receding, ebbing and flowing with the surge and swell of bodies merging, hearts connecting, until neither one was sure anymore where it was that she ended, and the other woman began.

By then they lay naked, twining together, transformed and clothed in nothing but an enchantment older even than the ocean. In that moment there were no shields and no secrets, no doubts or hesitation, only a mutual desire in which they consumed one another even as they gave everything that they had, everything that they were, asking nothing in return, and receiving everything. As the faint ocean sounds faded to be overcome by tender cries and soft moans, rising heartbeats and ancient rhythms, they met each other in the glory of cresting waves, riding the fiery pitch and roll of the waters with one pulse, with one fire, rocked to their very center with the power of the tides.

Their surroundings forgotten and their voices reduced to cries of pleasure, their desire soon intensified to a pitch that would not be controlled, not by the moon or by gravity, by seas or by shorelines, by one another or themselves, until the steady rhythm of the waves coalesced between them into an exquisite, powerful raging flood that swept them both away.

Spiraling slowly, lazily downward, the thunderous echoes of her release still washing through her, Kasey stretched languidly, her body thrumming with a quiet joy she had never known in all the years she had been alive. She felt loved, she felt cherished, she felt safe, and she knew the reason.

"Penny for your thoughts?" Lorelei whispered tenderly, the soft rush of her breath passing over the skin of Kasey's collarbone like a caress.

Kasey, who was scarcely yet capable of coherent thought, giggled softly, comfortable enough to confess the truth that at the moment her thinking was hardly deep or in any way insightful.

"Well if you must know," she answered, a tiny coil of heat flaring in her belly at the goosebumps that rose along Lorelei's arm at her whisper. "If you must know, I was thinking that I can't feel my toes."

The sound of Lorelei's phone rising in tinny echo through the open door to the living room underscored their laughter, and Lorelei smiled down at Kasey with a shake of her head. "I don't need to answer that," she said, perfectly willing and ready to ignore the real world forever if Kasey was.

Smiling, Kasey nudged her toward the edge of the mattress. "Maybe you should—Troy might need us."

Smiling back, Lorelei rose from the tumble of sheets and blankets like the Venus de Milo, unabashedly naked and painted in stained glass underwater rainbows.

"How do you know it's Troy?" she said, turning to fetch the phone from the living room as the strains of Lady Gaga's "Fashion" rose from its tiny speakers.

Kasey laughed. "Who else would you have given that ring tone?"

As Lorelei slipped from the bedroom to answer her cell phone, Kasey sat up in the bed, her knees to her chest and her arms around her legs. A soft brush of air—compliments of the air conditioning vents hidden beneath a free form ocean reef sculpture—caressed her bare shoulders, and she pressed her cheek to one drawn up knee, realizing contentedly that she had never in her life felt so happy.

Raising her gaze, she smiled as Lorelei appeared, framed in the doorway, the soft curves of her thighs and hips, breasts and belly bathed in underwater enchantment.

Lorelei did not smile back.

"What is it?" Kasey asked, a sudden frisson of worry rising inside her to spread through her limbs like an icy current.

"You were right, that was Troy," Lorelei said slowly, staring at the cell phone in her hand as if deciphering a puzzle. "But it was the strangest thing."

Kasey sat up straighter, Lorelei's clear concern meeting and merging with her own. "What did he say?"

"That's just it," Lorelei said worriedly, raising the cell phone to stare at it harder. "The call came from him, the caller ID said so, but he didn't say anything when I answered. I could sort of hear him breathing, I think, but that's all, and then when I called back, he didn't answer."

"Just breathing?" Kasey's expression turned quizzical. "Troy isn't the obscene phone call type," she pointed out the obvious. "Maybe it was a butt dial?"

Lorelei shook her head decidedly. "Troy isn't the butt dial type either," she said with surety. "He won't even carry a wallet in his pants pocket because it ruins the lines of his suit. He always has his wallet in his jacket and his phone in a holder on his belt."

Kasey rose from the bed and joined her in the doorway, both of them now staring at the phone as if demanding it give up its secrets.

"Do you think Troy is all right?" Kasey wondered aloud, her concern for their friend rising in her clearly worried features.

"I think," said Lorelei decisively, reaching for the articles of clothing both of them had strewn around the bedroom not an hour earlier, "that I'll feel better if we go over there and check on him."

Chapter Thirty One

On the way to Troy's condo in Kasey's old Nissan, Lorelei sat in the passenger seat, chewing fretfully on a teal-and-turquoise fingernail and drumming her other hand impatiently on the faded dashboard as they changed lanes for the third time in ten minutes. Muttering a curse underneath her breath as traffic stalled yet again, Bloomington's busy lunch hour flooding the streets with college students and local business people, she turned worried eyes to Kasey.

"I've called him back four times," she said, needing to speak the words even though Kasey had been sitting right beside her when she made the phone calls. "Why wouldn't he answer?"

"Please let him be in the bathroom focused on aftershave and hair product," Kasey murmured under her breath, unsure whether the wish was an incantation or a prayer. Troy was prodigiously perfectionist and fastidiously fashionable: it was quite possible that he was ignoring the phone in favor of a regimented session of meticulous male grooming. To keep herself from jumping to frightening conclusions, Kasey was determinedly picturing him shaping his eyebrows or moisturizing his cuticles or bleaching his already perfect teeth. Anything at all, anything except...

"You don't think that vile woman would have done something to him"? Lorelei spoke the thought that Kasey had been trying to avoid thinking, and as the words rose in the car between them, their gazes met in mutual, wide eyed worry.

"Maybe Troy should have been flirting with bodyguards instead of records clerks," Kasey muttered.

"Drive faster," Lorelei said hoarsely.

Spinning the steering wheel in a sudden curve that was completely reckless considering the amount of pedestrian traffic in the crosswalks, Kasey veered off the main street of town, cutting up and over and exceeding the speed limit with no regrets whatsoever. If a police officer had pulled her over at that very moment, she would have willingly agreed to go to the station in handcuffs so long as an officer—with lights and sirens and traffic immunity—was dispatched to Troy's condo first.

Turning sharply at the corner which housed the vintage clothing store where Troy bought 1940's silk ties and classic fedoras, Kasey blew through the parking garage of Troy's building like a tempest, barely acknowledging the attendant who guarded the elevator. Lorelei was right on her heels.

Troy's cell phone, blinking and filled with worried voice messages from Lorelei, was still in his hand when they found him, face down on the carpet where Reid Monteforte's hit-and-run muscle had left him. Whatever moment of lucidity had allowed him to draw the phone from its holder on his Italian leather belt and hit Lorelei's number on speed dial had abandoned him soon after, and he did not come to his senses again until he was ensconced in a hospital bed, hooked up to an IV and a monitor, and objecting loudly to the unfashionable and ill-fitting hospital gown he was wearing.

Resting a gentle hand on his shoulder, Lorelei soothed him quietly, promising to take him to Saks and Burberry at Fashion mall in Indianapolis if he would just let the afternoon nurse take his blood pressure without a fight. The nurse, jabbing him with a tranquilizer syringe and an irritated expression, solved the problem without her.

"He needs to rest," she said firmly, physically ushering Kasey and Lorelei out of the hospital room and closing the door behind them. "Come back later."

Standing out in the hallway, Kasey hugged her own elbows, the adrenaline that had driven her this far suddenly leaving the building without warning. "Now what?" she said, her voice forlorn and worried.

Lorelei set her pretty features in a determined expression. "We might as well go downstairs and get something to eat," she said, realizing that they had abandoned turkey sandwiches and salads in favor of a romantic assignation and never returned to them. "Then we're coming back up here and one of us is going to pretend to be his wife. They won't tell us anything otherwise."

Kasey shook her head but followed her into the elevator anyway. "They'll never believe he's straight," she said as the elevator doors closed behind them. "He smells much too nice for that."

The hospital cafeteria, a cavernous and well lit room with floor to ceiling windows on the outer wall, was surprisingly pleasant, with a massive salad bar, a cook-to-order grill and gourmet coffee choices. Sitting at a corner table, Kasey nursed a hazelnut latte and a roast beef sandwich, shaking her head as Lorelei set a silk patchwork backpack on the table beside her own sandwich and rested her hands on top of it. The backpack, purchased from a local artist's collective in the heart of Bloomington, had multiple pockets inside of it, each of which currently held a different suspicious and worrisome theory. Pulling the drawstring free and opening the backpack, Lorelei reached inside and drew a hastily folded paper from the silk lined interior, opening it and setting it between them on the table. Metaphorically stapled to the paper was her least favorite but most likely theory.

"Kasey," she said quietly, pushing aside her diet coke and smoothing out the paper, "this was on the floor next to Troy at the condo. I found it while we were waiting for the ambulance."

Eyes widening, Kasey pushed aside her tray of food, suddenly losing all appetite. The paper, a printout of the bids placed on the Belleview theatre property, was crumpled and spattered with dried red-brown stains, and she knew without asking that the blood belonged to Troy. At the bottom of the page, surrounded by more stains and dark ink smudges, a warning was scrawled in thick black marker, the words "Back Off" sending a clear and unequivocal message.

"It was on the floor right next to Troy," Lorelei said quietly, reaching across the table to take Kasey's hand in hers. "I think they wrapped his fingers around it before they left him there, whoever *they* are." She used her other hand to point at a faint set of smudges on the back of the paper. "Those look like fingerprints, don't they?"

Turning the crumpled paper over, Kasey tightened her own fingers around it, anger rising in a fierce and protective flood inside her chest.

"That's for the police to decide," she said in a low and brittle voice, admitting to herself for the first time that Troy might well have died on the floor of that condo before they got there. "This is bigger than us, now, Lorelei," she said fiercely, rising suddenly and pushing her uneaten food across the table. "There's no telling what these people are capable of."

Lorelei stood too, reaching to return the bloodstained paper to her backpack and facing Kasey across the table. "Troy isn't going to back off, and you and I both know it," she said quietly. "He's going to keep at this thing until something even worse happens, and whoever these people are, whatever they do to him, they aren't going to scare him away from it. He'll face them down alone if he has to."

"Yes, he will," Kasey said firmly, her expression set in a fiery determination Lorelei had never seen in her before. "That," she said, a fierce and passionate certainty painting her features in glorious conviction, "is why it's a good thing that Troy is not alone."

Smiling at last, the connection between them solidifying with common purpose and single-minded resolution, Lorelei nodded. Troy was a gossiping busybody, a matchmaking meddler and a frequent pain in the ass—but no matter what he did, he was *their* pain in the ass, and woe betide anybody who tried to hurt him.

Chapter Thirty Two

"Why didn't they stitch up that cut on the side of your head?" Lorelei pursed her lips, handing Troy another ice pack and setting her hands on her hips.

"Because I wouldn't let them cut my hair, of course," said Troy, wincing as he pressed the ice to his temple. "Lucky for me I woke up just before they tried it."

Lorelei shook her head, knowing it was futile to protest his priorities. Troy, who had checked himself out of the hospital against the orders of the doctor and taken an Uber home without telling Kasey or Lorelei, set his jaw at them, then winced.

"I couldn't stay in that hospital," he argued, though Lorelei had not voiced her opinion. "Did you see what they made me wear? Horrible." He sipped delicately from a bottle of San Pellegrino, still sulking. "They tried to feed me Jell-O."

Emerging from Troy's immaculate kitchen with a platter of crudités, gourmet cheeses, stone ground crackers and hummus, Kasey at least merited his approval. "You are an angel," Troy purred, capturing her hand with his and kissing the back of it. "Will you make me a martini?"

"No alcohol!" Lorelei protested, fully prepared to remind him that he had a concussion. "Didn't you read your discharge papers from the doctor?"

Troy flashed a decidedly coy set of dimples. "Of course not, darling," he said primly. "I have a concussion, I shouldn't strain my eyes."

Lorelei was not impressed. "Alcohol use after a concussion can damage your brain cells," she said, handing him a sheaf of hospital papers. "Not that you are currently using them."

Stepping between them before they started actually fighting, Kasey took Troy's hand in hers. "Troy, you need to rest. You got hurt and you need time to recuperate." She handed him a cracker. "Try to eat."

"What I need to do is deal with that legal weasel who sent her friends to ruin my suit with bloodstains," he said archly, gesturing toward the blood spattered paper Lorelei had set on the table. "She left her calling card, it would be rude not to respond."

Lorelei turned from the foyer where she had been wielding a screwdriver and a newly purchased door alarm. "Let me see that cut," she said, reaching toward the perfectly gelled strands of his now restored hairstyle. "I think your brain may have fallen out entirely."

Troy swatted her hand away, protecting his hair from both interrogation and ruffling. "Lorelei," he said, his expression turning serious, "They are trying to tear down Matteo's theatre, they are lying and cheating and stealing, and they sent their bully boys here to try to intimidate me. I'm not taking this lying down."

"Yes, you are," Lorelei said sternly, retrieving the papers he had tossed on the table and reading them aloud. "For the next three to five days at least, while taking your pills and drinking plenty of liquids."

Troy scowled. "Now you listen…" he started, but trailed off as Kasey seized his hand again, tears rising in her eyes.

"Troy," she said softly, her anguish at the thought of almost losing him clear on her features. "Troy, anything could have happened. Please rest. Please step back, just for a little while. Please do what the doctor told you to do. If anything happens to you it will break my heart. I love you."

Nonplussed, Troy opened his mouth, then closed it again. "I love you too, darling," he said finally, almost contrite yet clearly conniving. "But—"

"Kasey and I will follow the trail," Lorelei promised him suddenly, sitting on the coffee table and capturing his eyes with hers. "We'll follow leads, we'll ask questions, we'll look for clues while you are resting."

Troy settled back against the sofa cushions sulkily but winced as the movement jostled his head. For a moment he assumed a stubborn expression, then wilted, suddenly capitulating. "I will eat soup," he conceded grandly, clearly a noble and suffering martyr making the ultimate sacrifice. "I will consume dry toast and submit to pampering. But only until tomorrow morning." He ostentatiously set an alarm on the state of the art watch he wore on his left wrist. "After that we fight for the theatre and we let nothing stop us."

Lorelei's worried expression deepened. "You won't ever let this go, will you?" she asked him ruefully.

Troy sat up against his pillows, every trace of cajoling and sarcasm fading from his features. "It is the hill I will die on," he said quietly.

"That's what I'm afraid of," said Lorelei, rising to take his empty San Pellegrino bottle back to the kitchen and hide a few tears of her own.

"We won't fail," Troy said to Kasey, who still sat on the edge of the sofa, once again holding onto his hand as though she could keep him safe just by wishing.

"How do you know?" she asked plaintively.

"Darling," Troy smiled, wincing again as the movement caused his battered lip to resume bleeding. "We won't fail because we are the good guys."

Chapter Thirty Three

Despite his stubborn assertion that he was fine and perfectly capable of taking on crooked lawyers, hired bullies and dangerous mysteries, Troy fell asleep halfway through the lobster bisque, French bread and gruyere he had insisted be delivered after Kasey failed to find cans of chicken noodle soup or crackers in his cupboards. Lorelei put a blanket over him and left him where he was on the sofa, finally satisfied that he was resting. Sighing with worry, she drew Kasey out onto Troy's balcony, setting two gracefully curvaceous wrought iron chaise lounges together and settling Kasey on one of them before lowering herself onto the other. She kept one eye trained through the sliding glass doors on their recalcitrant but once again fashionable patient.

Like Troy, the furniture on the balcony tended toward the graceful and ostentatious, and she set two cold beers and Troy's unfinished cheese and baguette down on the matching wrought iron table between the lounges. Screened from the neighboring balconies by gracious, tree like plants in massive terra cotta pots, the scene was idyllic, quiet and peaceful, a mix of golden sun and dappled shade, shifting and sighing in the afternoon breezes. Reluctantly, Lorelei broke the quiet.

"It's a shame we've run out of people to flirt with," she said mournfully, stretching her legs out and wriggling her bare toes in their strappy sandals. "I promised him we would follow the trail, but it isn't as though we actually have a trail to follow."

Kasey shook her head, reaching across the space between the chairs and taking her hand. "You were trying to make him feel better," she said stoutly, releasing Lorelei's fingers to tear off a piece of French bread and offer it to her like a security blanket of stone ground flour and gruyere. "It was only a white lie, not even that. A grey lie. Not even really a lie at all, just a stretchy sort of truth."

Despite her worry over Troy, over the situation, Lorelei laughed suddenly, accepting the bread and leaning over to kiss Kasey lightly on the lips. "Thank God that you found me," she said, leaning back against the designer textiles accenting Troy's patio furniture, "or I would've spent my whole life thinking I'm just a garden variety liar."

Kasey smiled weakly, thinking fleetingly that Lorelei would never spout the sort of lies that promised love and loyalty and devotion when those promises were already being broken. Tightening her lips, she shook her head faintly, the gesture a deliberate decision to not judge all women—especially this woman—by the actions of Cassandra and her ilk. Cassandra was a faithless cheat and her new girlfriend was terrifying, but Lorelei was something else altogether and Kasey was determined to look at her with open eyes and an open heart, and not let the betrayal in her past spoil her chance for future happiness.

When Cassandra had admitted (with no visible shame or remorse) that she had not been faithful, Kasey had sworn she would never risk her heart again. At the time she had thought that any attempt to love or trust another woman after Cassandra's cruel and casual dismissal would have been too great a leap, too difficult an endeavor, and she had relegated the idea to the realm of the impossible, packing it in layers of newspaper and taping it up in a box stored away in a metaphorical attic, never to be opened again.

Marveling quietly, grateful, she glanced sideways at Lorelei, who had stretched her arms above her head, arching the stress out of her back and turning her face to the sun. Eyes closed, breathing softly, she held the pose a moment as if half yoga, half fairy tale sculpture, and Kasey held her breath to watch her, realizing suddenly that Lorelei had rendered the impossible possible, and that love and trust and new beginnings were suddenly as simple as reaching across the space between two chairs on a balcony. Smiling softly, Kasey reached.

Part of what made Lorelei so wonderful, she mused, was her ability to love—unconditionally, almost unintentionally—without demands or expectations or reservations. The way she cared for Troy, the gentle understanding she offered to his hidden pain and his unadmitted heartache, would have told Kasey all she needed to know even if she had not discovered the essence of Lorelei's heart for herself. Nodding in recognition, she acknowledged that she and Lorelei would have had Troy in common even if they had not connected in every other way. Neither one of them knew how to ease his pain, but both were willing to help him carry it without making him admit how heavy it actually was.

Sighing quietly, the soft sound akin the coo of a dove, Kasey again turned her thoughts to the conundrum of helping Troy, sitting up suddenly as an obvious but unpleasant idea crossed her mind without asking permission.

"W-we haven't actually run out of people to flirt with," she stammered suddenly, as Lorelei opened her tired eyes and sat up beside her, her hand still linked with Kasey's.

"Who do we have left to flirt with?" she said cautiously, two small lines appearing between her eyebrows at the worried expression Kasey was wearing. "Kasey?"

Swallowing the disconcertingly large lump that had formed in her throat, Kasey reminded herself that Troy had always been there for her (mermaid tails and seafood platters aside) and that she wanted to be there for Troy.

"My ex-girlfriend, Cassandra," she reminded Lorelei quietly, forcing aside the tightening of her chest at what she was about to suggest. "She's dating that awful lawyer. I could talk to her and see what she knows. There's no telling what that woman might have told her."

Lorelei dropped her hand for a moment, spinning around on the chaise lounge and planting her feet on the concrete. "Would your ex-girlfriend have had anything to do with Troy getting hurt?" she asked tightly, reaching for Kasey's hand again and leaning forward.

"Cassandra and Troy never got along," Kasey said slowly, raising her other hand to brush a long, sleek strand of hair back behind her ear, "but I don't think she would have had anything to do with…" she glanced back through the sliding glass doors to the living room, her expression troubled, remembering that she had misjudged Cassandra before. Setting her expression, she turned back to face Lorelei. "Well the fastest way to find out is to ask, isn't it?" she said helplessly, cringing at the idea of facing Cassandra, but suddenly determined to do it.

She was, after all, no longer Cassandra's cast-off little waif, betrayed and heartbroken, humiliated, adrift and abandoned. She was a woman in love. In love with someone who loved her in return. She was trying to help a true and loyal friend who had never let her down, she had her head most firmly above water and she was standing on her own two fins. She was in a relationship with a sea siren. She was cherished and appreciated, supported and treasured. She was, in point of fact, a freaking mermaid, and she wasn't going to be intimidated by a bottom dweller like Cassandra Carat, that's what.

Smiling suddenly, the worry lines disappearing from her forehead, Lorelei watched the thoughts moving across Kasey's face, seeing fear and intimidation being shown the door by confidence and determination and spirit. She had never seen anything—or any one—so beautiful in her life.

"You are so far above the likes of her, of both of them," she said, drawing Kasey forward into a kiss that lingered. "She was a fool to let you go."

Smiling a sudden saucy smile almost worthy of Troy, Kasey nodded. "She was."

Lorelei leaned closer and kissed her again, her arms pulling Kasey from one chair to the other and drawing her across her knees. Sliding against parted thighs and tanned, scented skin, the long white skirt Lorelei wore pushed itself into gathers beneath Kasey, a soft, silky cushion between bohemian grace and boots-and-blue-jeans, the thin fabric doing nothing to mask the sudden yearning of their bodies for each other.

"Well she isn't getting you back," Lorelei whispered into the seashell curve of Kasey's ear, her arm sliding around the trim waist and curved hips that had settled into a position she intended for them to occupy forever. "Not now that I've found you. You're my treasure now."

Reaching with her other hand, she drew a ribbon from around her neck, passing it over Kasey's head and carefully lifting the long dark strands of hair free from its embrace. Suspended from the ribbon was a silver pendant in the shape of a mermaid tail, etched with fanciful designs and engraved with words in swirling, curving letters. Tipping her head sideways, Kasey lifted the pendant to read what it said.

No fear of deep water

"If you're going to go talk to her," Lorelei said, wishing Kasey wouldn't, but respecting her right to make her own decision, "wear this so you can take me with you."

"I do take you with me," Kasey whispered back, har arms sliding around Lorelei's neck as though they had been there always. "Everywhere I go."

Caught up in a kiss as passionate and perfect as the roaring of the ocean, Lorelei was able to spare only the briefest of moments to be grateful for the tall potted plants that screened the balcony from sight. After all, it wouldn't have done to shock Troy's neighbors while he was sleeping.

Chapter Thirty Four

If Kasey was surprised when Cassandra agreed to meet her at a wine bar in downtown Bloomington, she did her best not to show it. Cassandra—who had flatly refused to set a designer shod foot in the coffee house—might have agreed out of spite, or simply for the opportunity to gloat, but Kasey didn't care. There were more important things in life than Cassandra's petty revenge, and Troy and Lorelei were two of them.

The wine bar, an upscale establishment high on dark wood and dim lighting and low on affordable pricing, wasn't Kasey's cup of tea (in fact she would have preferred a simple cup of tea) but she slid into the elegant booth, setting her purse on the fine leather seat beside her and wearing Lorelei's necklace like a talisman. She had been hurt by Cassandra, humiliated and cast aside, but the other side of the coin was much shinier and brighter. She was now loved by a beautiful mermaid and was still friends with a handsome prince being heroic in the name of true love: it made her courageous and strong. Cassandra could not hurt her anymore.

"So, what was so important that I had to come downtown to discuss it with you?" Cassandra said archly, pouring a second glass from a very expensive vintage. "I have other things to do."

"I know you're busy," Kasey said quietly, touching the pendant she wore at her throat to remind herself that she was loved and cherished, and not by the cold, antagonistic woman seated across from her at the table. "Thanks for agreeing to meet with me."

Tightening her shoulders, Cassandra pictured herself for an uncomfortable moment, crouched under the desk in Reid's office, performing a service and being rewarded with a shopping spree. She shrugged off the feeling the memory gave her, but the discomfort of it lingered. It was too much like Reid leaving money on the bedside table after hiring an escort.

"Whatever," she said shortly, draining the glass of wine far faster than the sommelier had suggested. "Spit it out, Kasey."

Spreading her fingers on the table and taking courage from Lorelei's firm and specific assurance that she was worth a hundred of opportunistic Cassandra and her evil bitch girlfriend, Kasey took a deep breath.

"Cassandra, Troy is trying to save the Belleview theatre…" she started, trailing off as Cassandra seized the bottle of wine and poured herself another.

"No kidding," she said, her voice bitter and sarcastic. "Reid is furious."

"That's what I wanted to talk to you about," Kasey went on, wondering suddenly what she had ever seen in Cassandra. "Troy was attacked at his condo yesterday and he wound up in the hospital. I think your girlfriend had something to do with it."

The wine glass, held in Cassandra's freshly manicured fingers, jerked suddenly, drops of wine tumbling over the edge to stain the pristine damask of the tablecloth.

"What?" Her voice was shocked, angry, filled with outrage, but her expression was suddenly pensive.

Kasey stood her ground. "On the floor next to Troy, whoever hurt him left a copy of the auction printout for the theatre, with the words 'back off' written on the bottom. The only other bid for the property was your girlfriend's law firm."

"That's ridiculous!" Cassandra sputtered, setting the wine glass back on the table. "You'd better be careful throwing around accusations like that, Kasey, defamation could get you into legal trouble."

Kasey, who had to admit that Cassandra knew a great deal more about law than she did, shook her head.

"Look, Cassandra, I know you're in a relationship with Reid Monteforte, and that is none of my business...anymore," she said firmly, the pause both deliberate and damning. "But I think you need to ask whether you really want to ally yourself with the kind of person who would put a stranger in the hospital simply because he might get in the way of something she wanted."

"Reid didn't *do* that, Kasey!" Cassandra exploded, her heart suddenly beating faster with the question of whether or not that was true. Uneasily, she recalled the cell phone conversation she had overheard in Reid's elegant office.

"Maybe not," Kasey conceded, leaving her own wine glass untouched on the table in front of her, "but what if she paid someone else to do it?"

"You watch too many bad movies," Cassandra said scornfully, horrified by the thought that her ex-girlfriend might be speaking the truth. "This is the real world, you know. Things happen."

"Things *did* happen!" Kasey answered sharply, recalling with frustration the police explanation that it would take weeks of backlog before they could even test the paper for usable fingerprints. "Whoever they were, they left him lying on the floor of his condo, bleeding. They beat him unconscious over a piece of real estate, Cassandra, then they just *left* him there." She gripped the edge of the table with her fingers, the green and blue glass beads on a bracelet Lorelei had made her glinting faintly in the dim light.

"Oh, grow up, Kasey," Cassandra snapped, reaching to pay for the bottle of wine with Reid's credit card. Signing the slip with an indecipherable flourish, she rose from the table, and Kasey found herself wondering whether she had learned to forge signatures from Reid herself. Pausing in the middle of a dramatic exit Cassandra hovered, silent for a moment before speaking.

"Is Troy going to be okay?" she asked tersely.

Straightening her spine, Kasey raised an eyebrow and stared her down. "Do you really care?"

Cassandra left without answering.

Chapter Thirty Five

Short of having Troy's phone surgically removed from his fingers, there was little Lorelei could do to keep him from having contact with the outside world, but she did her best to insulate him from the pain of current events. Her efforts, well intentioned and less than subtle, did not prevent him from reading an e-mail informing him that in the absence of the promised (and nonexistent) funds he had bid on the Belleview theatre, the auction had awarded the sale of the property to the law firm of Monteforte, Price and Riskin.

"I'm not taking my eyes off of you," Lorelei warned, wrestling him for the cell phone and losing. "The doctor said you need to rest and that's what you're going to do."

"Are you worried I'll stage an escape?" Troy said, pronouncing it 'es-cop-ay' and making it sound like an expensive bottle of wine. "Do you really think I would leave the house in this?" He gestured toward the decidedly expensive silk pajamas he was wearing.

Lorelei nodded. "Yes. And you'd make it look good too."

Troy smiled cunningly back at her. "But these bandages," he lamented. "They're *so* last season."

Lorelei pointed him stubbornly back toward the sofa. "Park it. And take your pills."

Sighing dramatically, Troy capitulated, tucking the pain pill in his cheek instead of swallowing it. "Quiet now, girl," he ordered grandly, waving the television remote at the flat screen. "My stories are on."

"Grumpy old man," Lorelei teased him, invoking every one of the scant years that separated their ages. She yawned broadly, wishing he would fall asleep so that she could do the same. "I was up half the night taking care of you."

"Get off my lawn," Troy grumbled in response, spitting the pill into his hand when she wasn't looking.

"You need to eat something," Lorelei fussed, moving to the kitchen and examining Troy's empty cupboards. "Don't you shop?"

"I've been much too busy chaining myself to theatre doors and getting beat up," Troy said, assuming a tragic expression that quickly turned wily. "Owww…" He dragged the single syllable out for maximum sympathy points.

Returning from the kitchen, Lorelei put her hands on her hips, well aware she was once again being railroaded by dimples and the devil. "Will you eat if I go get you something?"

"Coffee and cannoli," Troy said readily, "but only from Karma Sumatra."

"That's twenty minutes from here!" Lorelei protested.

Troy, too, had done the math. "But Jorge always makes it for me special," he wheedled, leaning back against the sofa cushions and trying to look pale beneath his salon tan. "And I'm in pain!"

Lorelei pointed a finger. "You *are* a pain," she corrected him, though she was already capitulating.

"You can take my car," Troy offered, his expression turning saintly.

"Oh, I'm going to," Lorelei assured him. "And you'd better not have moved from that sofa when I get back!"

"I love you, darling!" Troy protested at her retreating back, insinuating but not promising that he would obey her instructions. He was up and calling a taxi by the time she had left the parking garage, and long gone by the time she returned.

Chapter Thirty Six

Leaving the wine bar and driving back across town to the penthouse apartment where she was living with Reid, Cassandra found she could not get the sound of Kasey's final question out of her head. Though she had made it clear that she was no longer interested in being in a relationship with Kasey, Cassandra found that for the first time in a long time, Kasey's opinion of her mattered, at least a little. The truth was that Cassandra didn't know the answer to Kasey's question, and not knowing bothered her more than she wanted to admit. Did she care what happened to Troy? Shouldn't she care? Had she become the sort of person who no longer cared if a man had been beaten and maybe even left for dead?

Cassandra and Troy had never gotten along, this was a fact known by anyone who had ever been in a room with the two of them for more than five minutes. In addition to being diametrically opposed on nearly every single subject worth an argument, Troy had constantly harped on Cassandra about the way she treated Kasey, and Cassandra had just as constantly reminded Troy to mind his own damn business. He didn't of course—that was Troy in a designer labelled nutshell—full of opinions and in everybody else's business. It had always driven Cassandra crazy. But now, just a little, stinging from the way that Reid so frequently brushed her off, Cassandra was beginning to look at the way she had treated Kasey with a new set of eyes. In those eyes, operating from a suddenly different perspective, she found herself beginning to wonder whether Troy might actually have had a point. Of course, that was Troy too—he *always* had a point, and he was always making it. But that didn't mean that he deserved to get hurt, to have his home invaded, to be threatened and beaten and left on the floor of his condo, bleeding and unconscious.

Shivering for a moment, Cassandra tried to push the image from her mind, wishing Kasey had not described it. For a moment she felt a surge of relief that she would not acknowledge, as the tightening in her chest and the disquiet of her thoughts proved that perhaps she was not as heartless as she had feared.

Turning the car into the security guarded garage beneath Reid's expensive, elegant building, she pulled into in a reserved parking space and gathered her things together, crossing the neatly paved area between the parking spaces and the elevator. Punching in the security code that kept the wealthy residents of the building from ever being exposed to the elements or the neighbors, she rode the elevator up and up, deciding during the trip that it couldn't hurt to simply ask Reid about the attack on Troy Preston. Shivering again, she stepped out of the elevator and into the sumptuous foyer of Reid's apartment, realizing with a sudden sense of unease that she was wrong. It might very well hurt a great deal.

Reid was home, but predictably working on the weekend, a pair of sleek black lacquer glasses perched on the top of her perfectly coiffed head, and a deep red manicure decorating the index finger tapping impatiently on a sheaf of papers. She looked up when Cassandra entered, and reached almost unconsciously for the wine glass at her elbow, the ruby liquid reminding Cassandra uncomfortably of blood, and Troy lying on the floor of his condo. Shuddering, she pushed the picture aside.

"Reid, I'm glad you're home," she said, squaring her shoulders and setting down her purse.

Flashing a smile that held neither warmth nor amusement, Reid tossed the glasses to the table and pushed her paperwork to one side. "Did you pick up the lingerie I ordered for you?" she said, rising from her chair to perch on the edge of the table when Cassandra nodded. "Put it on," she ordered, "so I can take it off you."

"Reid," Cassandra started, trailing off as her girlfriend rose from the table, one perfectly sculpted eyebrow rising in annoyance.

"You always talk too much, Pussycat," Reid murmured, her low voice vaguely threatening. "Haven't we discussed this?"

Crossing the room in long strides, she took the tissue filled shopping bag from Cassandra's unresisting fingers and drew out a handful of red and black silk, dangling an expensive teddy from one finger by a thin, diaphanous strap. "I have to be somewhere in an hour," she said bluntly, holding the garment in front of Cassandra's face. "Shouldn't you be getting naked?"

Drawing a deep breath and holding it for a moment, Cassandra made a decision. "Can we talk?" she asked hesitantly, taking a step back from both Reid and the lingerie she held in imperious fingers.

Stilettos clicking on the marble floor, Reid closed the distance between them. "Sure, Pussycat," she said, snaking an arm around Cassandra's waist and pulling her sharply against her body. She bent to press her lips against Cassandra's neck, her high end matte lipstick specifically designed to stay in place despite kissing and…other things. "Make an appointment."

When Cassandra did not capitulate, did not respond, did not immediately melt against the two thousand dollar red dress and designer push up bra, the kiss turned into a bite that was neither seductive nor subtle. Gasping, Cassandra pushed free, fingers rising to her neck, where a red welt was already rising.

"Reid, do you know anything about Troy Preston and the Belleview theatre?" she blurted suddenly, Reid's blood colored dress and lipstick and manicure making her think unflatteringly of vampires. "Someone went to his condo yesterday and put him in the hospital."

Freezing for a moment, Reid's expression suddenly hardened, and Cassandra felt a faint flutter of something that tasted an awful lot like fear.

"Oh dear. Poor Pussycat," Reid murmured caustically, her usually seductive mouth pursed in an expression of false distress. "Have we been talking to mermaids?" The red and black teddy slipped from her fingers and fell to the floor.

Swallowing the lump that seemed to have lodged in her throat, Cassandra took another step back.

"Reid," she whispered, the words rising in the sudden, icy silence to shatter against a wall of indifference. "Did you have something to do with what happened to Troy?"

Taking a step toward her, Reid set her expression. "Let's get one thing straight, Cassandra," she said, spitting out the name as if she didn't like the taste. "I am going to buy that theatre and the land that it sits on, and I am going to crush anyone that gets in the way of me doing it."

Cassandra drew her breath in sharply. "But—what about your clients?" she sputtered, falling silent at a cruel chuckle from her girlfriend.

"Completely fabricated," Reid said in a tone that made it clear she thought Cassandra was an idiot. "The theatre property was going to be my acquisition from the beginning, and it sure as hell is going to be my acquisition now. I don't really care what it takes to make it happen."

Cassandra's eyes widened, but Reid took no notice. "I'm going to develop the property in a year or two, when the records I falsified aren't under so much scrutiny," she was positively gloating. "But I'm knocking that building down today."

Horrified, Cassandra shook her head. "But—but why?" her voice, plaintive and shocked, sounded weak even in her own ears.

Reid smiled a deadly, silky smile. "Because I'm a bitch like that," she explained without a shred of regret. She bent to scoop up a luxurious handful of the exorbitantly expensive lingerie she preferred her lovers to wear, and tossed it at Cassandra, who caught it out of reflex.

"Part of the problem or part of the solution, my girl," she said coldly, "and you are not a part of the solution. Get out."

Crossing the room to the doorway, she took Cassandra's key ring from the table by the door and calmly removed the key to the apartment.

"Keep the teddy, Cassandra," she said, her voice thick with scorn and condescension. "I'll buy my next girl a new one."

Dazed, Cassandra picked up her purse and turned toward the doorway, pausing as Reid's voice rose one last time from the foyer. "One way or another, I am going to eliminate the problem of Troy Preston, permanently," the cold voice threatened. "Don't get in my way, Cassandra, or I will run you over too."

Chapter Thirty Seven

Unlike Cassandra, Kasey left the wine bar with no crisis of conscience or moral ambivalence regarding the subject of Troy. She might have trusted too much, too soon, in the wrong sort of people in the past, but now—safe and secure in Lorelei and the connection both of them were feeling—all of her energies were attuned to loyalty, to love, to truth and justice and doing what was right whether or not it was easy. It was not about situational ethics, or split loyalties, or selfish motivations, it was about love and friendship, and being there when somebody needed it. Admittedly there might have been times in the past when Kasey wanted to stab Troy with a silver plated fish fork, but nobody else had better try it.

Gripping the steering wheel of the Nissan with frustrated hands, she pulled into the small parking lot behind Karma Sumatra, deciding in the moment to bring coffee back for Lorelei and Troy. If she could not bring them information or confirmation (and Cassandra had been forthcoming with neither) at least she could bring them sugar, foam and espresso shots—she supposed it was better than nothing.

Hurrying around the corner, down three steps and through the purple door that led to the front room of Karma Sumatra, she slid to a sudden stop on the black-and-white checkered tile, nearly dropping the twenty dollar bill she had fished out of her pocket. At the counter, elbows bent and head tipped in concentration, Lorelei was discussing the finer points of Troy-wrangling with Jorge while Florence put the finishing touches on coffee cups and pastry boxes.

"Lorelei!" Kasey cried, crossing the room with swift, shocked steps, her innocent expression horrified. "What are you doing here? Who is babysitting Troy!"

Lorelei's expression, which had lit up at the sight of Kasey, fell suddenly. "He was hungry!" she protested weakly, reaching belatedly for the pastry box Florence was handing her. "There wasn't any food in the condo!"

Jorge shook his head, a sly smile taking over his features. "Did he tell you that?" he said, patting Lorelei on the shoulder. "You know that boy is lying to you, right?"

"Th-the cupboards were empty!" Lorelei protested, looking wildly back and forth between Kasey and Jorge as Florence shook her head and flipped the towel she carried over one shoulder.

Jorge laughed, his teeth bright against the deliberately sexy dark stubble that covered his cheeks and chin. "He keeps the food in the pantry, Lorelei," he pointed out the obvious. "Reaching up to the cupboards rumples his dress shirts, and you know how he feels about *that*!"

Lorelei was horrified. "We have to get back to the condo!" she cried, already spinning toward the doorway. Snatching up the coffee cups and cannoli box, she fled in the direction of the on-street parking, where Troy's pampered little car reclined in vintage, polished splendor beside the meter at the curb.

Leaning on the counter, Jorge shook his head at Kasey. "Take care of him, Chica," he said with a pensive smile. "You and I both know he's crazy."

The condo was empty when they got there, and Kasey knew that they should not have been surprised. Jorge had been right. Nonplussed, Lorelei sank down on the sofa and pulled out her phone, preparing a speech that would have made Troy's ears burn if he had answered his cell phone, which he didn't.

Kasey hovered near the kitchen doorway. "What if those people came back?" she asked apprehensively, opening a door in the wall to discover that Troy had enough groceries to feed a hungry army. "What if something happened to him?"

Rising to fling open the door to Troy's bedroom for the second time (he had not spontaneously reappeared) Lorelei stormed the ensuite bathroom to find the silk pajamas he had been wearing fastidiously folded on a leather upholstered bench next to the jacuzzi bathtub, and his hairbrush and razor lined up neatly on the counter. Wherever he had vanished to, Troy had done it under his own power, and ensured that he looked good while doing it: a hint of cologne still lingered on the hand towels.

"Troy has flown the coop," Kasey observed unnecessarily from the doorway, Troy's car keys already in her fingers. "And we both know where he's flown to."

While Kasey drove at breakneck speed in the direction of the Belleview theatre, Lorelei called Troy another half dozen times from the passenger seat of the convertible. Finally answering his phone, unrepentant and deliberately breezy, Troy granted them only a dozen words before hanging up and refusing to answer again.

"I can't talk now darling, there's a bulldozer trying to squash me."

Careening around the corner with a recklessness born of justified alarm, Kasey slid the car to a stop to find Troy standing in front of the theatre, literally staving off a bulldozer and wrecking ball while wearing charcoal grey virgin wool Versace.

Reid Monteforte stood across the sidewalk from him, a towering cobra in Dolce and Gabbana.

"Proceed," she said coldly to the man operating the massive bulldozer that loomed dangerously over Troy. "He'll move out of the way. He won't let you run over him, he can't be that stupid."

"I most certainly can!" Troy bellowed, once again gripping the burnished brass twin doorknobs and pretending he was holding Matteo's hands. God, how he missed those hands, that heart, that light, that courage. But, he vowed, he would do Matteo's memory proud. This woman was trying to destroy his beloved's legacy for nothing more than greed and profit, and Troy was not going to let that happen. It simply would not stand.

Nodding in the direction of Kasey and Lorelei, who arrived on the scene out of breath and horrified, he fixed his expression and pointed it at the enemy. Seething and poisonous, Reid stared back at him, neither one of them blinking.

Breaking the standoff, the driver—shaken by Reid's assertion that he should plow Troy over with the bulldozer—threw down his hard hat in disgust.

"Lady," he said, shifting the massive piece of machinery into reverse, "if you want to kill a man over a freaking building, you can do it yourself. I quit."

Clenching her jaw, Reid held Troy's antagonistic glare for another long moment, before signaling to the limousine that once again hovered at the corner, covered this time in a fine sheen of dust from the passing bulldozer as it turned in the intersection and disappeared from sight.

"This is not over," she spat at Troy, hurling her handbag onto the seat behind the dark tinted windows and following its trajectory. "I promise you, you will not win this war." The door slammed behind her, and Troy kept his gaze fixed on the limousine until it finally disappeared in the distance.

"But I did win this battle," he said quietly, releasing the door handles just in time to topple into Lorelei's arms. Hurrying to help support him, Kasey seized a flawlessly ironed elbow.

"Oh Troy," she murmured into his ear, half holding, half hugging him as they helped him to the car. "I love you, but you're an idiot."

Chapter Thirty Eight

Weak and exhausted, as pale as the clouds that drifted by outside the window, Troy deigned to remove his tie and suit jacket, but put down a well shod foot and dug in his heels when Lorelei tried to make him put on his pajamas.

"I need this suit," he protested weakly, lowering himself onto the sofa with a sharp grimace of pain that reminded Kasey that he shouldn't have been out of the hospital at all. Troy tucked a hand into her elbow. "It's my armor," he explained, resting painfully back against the pillows, a wounded knight only catching his breath before riding back into battle.

Exchanging glances with Lorelei, Kasey patted his shoulder. "It's Sunday, Troy," she comforted sensibly, reaching for the bottle of pain pills he had not taken. "She won't be able to get another contractor out there today. You need to rest."

Troy, who had been given marching orders in one direction or the other (either home or the hospital) wilted in visible relief at her words, and Lorelei moved from her spot blocking the doorway to sit on the other side of him.

"Troy," she said tenderly, "what can we do to help you?"

Raising blue eyes, bloodshot with dark circles underscoring the pale skin of his face, Troy shuddered suddenly, a wave of pain passing through him that had little to do with cracked ribs, cuts and bruises. He looked lost, bleak and broken; weary and wounded and literally unable to stand. Horrified, Lorelei saw the truth take him by the throat, and watched the fight go out of him.

"I can't do it," he whispered, his grief pouring out like a tempest held too long behind solid iron bars. "I can't save Matteo."

Kasey seized his hand in hers, feeling her own heart breaking with the pain of his. "Matteo's theatre, you mean," she corrected softly, but Troy shook his head even as he squeezed her fingers.

"I couldn't save Matteo either," he said, tears spilling over and leaving streaks across his face that he didn't bother to hide. "I couldn't save him, and I tried." He drew back his hand, burying his face in his fingers as sobs began wracking his body. "I begged to take his place in that damned hospital bed, I begged to take his pain away, I begged to be the one to die so I wouldn't have to live without him."

Kasey rested her fingers on his knee, where tears of pain had left tiny spatters against the grey of the fine cloth. "You begged who?" she asked gently.

"I don't know!" Troy burst out, long past any semblance of hiding his anguish behind designer clothes and conversation. That strategy had run its course and could no longer uphold him. Even his inveterate matchmaking now seemed like a ploy to distract him from his grieving.

"I begged God. Fate. The whole goddamn universe." He covered his face with his hands again, gasping out breath after breath until it seemed he would come apart entirely, whatever seams that held him together snapping under the strain of keeping his sorrow inside him.

Rubbing his back in gentle circles, Lorelei waited, patient and loving, until the storm seemed to be passing. Watching her, Kasey was struck again by her kindness, her gentle heart, her fierce loyalty to the people she cared about. Realizing that she, too, was included in that love, in that loyalty, she breathed a quiet prayer of thanks, even as she breathed a prayer of comfort for her friend.

Beneath Lorelei's hand, Troy was finally stirring, speaking, his voice a cracked and broken whisper. "I'll eat, I'll sleep, I promise," he said hoarsely, turning pain filled eyes to stare at them, "I'll even take my damn pills. Just please…please leave me alone."

Transfixed by his surrender, unable to bear his sorrow, Lorelei and Kasey stared at one another for a long moment, knowing that the kindest thing they could do in that moment was to give him space to mourn in.

"I won't put my phone down all day," Lorelei said quietly, as Kasey rose to kiss Troy on the forehead and make her way to the door. "You call if you need anything at all."

Rising, she fussed with the throw pillows, straightening the magazines on the end table, folding a blanket over his knees, filling a glass of water and leaving it at his elbow. Finally, unable to do anything more to ease his pain or his heartache, they gave him what he had asked for.

Chapter Thirty Nine

As Lorelei and Kasey stepped into the elevator, Troy rose from the sofa, soul sick and heartsore, too filled with grief to even lock the door behind them. Pulling on the jacket of his fine suit, he drifted painfully into the bedroom and crossed the carpet to the lonely double bed, resting his body at last against the mattress and pillows. Turning his face from the light of the window, he stared across the room at his dresser, where the box of Matteo's letters rested in the top drawer, a hidden treasure that represented all he had lost, but that celebrated all he had known. Losing the man that he loved had been indescribably, impossibly painful, but Troy knew without any shadow of doubt that to have the years he had shared with Matteo, he would have suffered the loss of losing him a hundred times over. Some things were worth any amount of pain.

Rising slowly, he stumbled across the room to the dresser and pulled out the letters, realizing in a slow and bittersweet revelation that Matteo's memory could not, did not, reside in a wooden box, a burning candle and a set of envelopes. It resided where it had always resided, kept safe and surrounded, in the heart of the man he had loved. Making a decision as painful as it was cathartic, Troy reached out a shaky hand and lifted the flickering candle in its frosted glass holder, raising it to his face and staring for a moment into the flame, before softly blowing it out and setting it down.

"Goodbye," he whispered, stepping back and sinking onto the bed as though his legs could no longer support him. Opening the box, he drew the familiar letters out and set them on the bedspread, holding the final letter in tender fingers for a moment before turning the envelope over. Sliding a well tended fingernail beneath the flap, he inhaled painfully, the trapped scent of long ago cologne rising almost imperceptibly from the paper beneath his fingers, faint traces of what had once been love and warmth and heat and heart and hands. Almost trembling, he heard a soft sigh rising in the quiet air of the bedroom without realizing it was his own. Acknowledging its sorrow, recognizing its pain, he heard it drift into silence. Raising his eyes slowly, he held the opened envelope for a moment, the broken seal and release of memories the last he would ever know of the man whose soul he had treasured.

He was surprised to see that the room looked no different, that the world still kept turning, that outside the condo, life continued for millions upon millions of other people, few of whom knew or would even care that one man's heart lay shattered on the well vacuumed pile of a tastefully color coordinated carpet. The heart, of course, had broken two years earlier, but Troy had gathered and kept every single one of the pieces. It was not that he ever intended to use the pieces again: it was that those pieces, numbered and counted and carefully tended, belonged to Matteo, would always belong to Matteo, given to him freely and forever, and held in perpetuity. Troy would not have dreamed of taking them back.

Glancing around the room, he shook his head, still surprised to find that it looked no different than it had a moment before. He had thought that the sunlight coming in through the windows might be duller, somehow, the shadows dancing on the wall stilled in their movements, the extinguishing of that tiny little candle flame bringing darkness to rooms and hallways, draining color from flowers and furniture, leaving behind only heartache when it flickered out and floated away, a tiny wisp of smoke the only thing left of its two year vigil.

"I'm sorry, my love," Troy whispered in the silence. "I tried. I swear that I tried."

Chapter Forty

When Troy slipped his fingers inside the envelope that bore Matteo's last letter, he expected to find professions of love, promises of forever, a painting or poetry and the pain of knowing that never again would he open an envelope to discover what Matteo had placed for him inside. What he did not expect was a sheaf of legal papers, several official documents, and a heavy silver key.

Opening the papers—a two year old deed of sale and multiple property related documents—he stared, uncomprehending for a moment, as he tried to make sense of what he was holding. In the envelope, a painful reminder of the impermanence of living, was a copy of Matteo's will, the same will enacted two years earlier, leaving everything Matteo had—his possessions, his property and his undying devotion—to Troy. The document was not unfamiliar. Troy had gone over it in painful detail with Matteo's lawyers and his family, had been the executor of Matteo's estate, had even tried to bargain with God to give back every cent for just one more day with his beloved, to no avail. But the other documents, paper copies of the transaction records which had been erased from the official database, had been placed in that envelope for Troy's eyes alone. In his hand, stamped and signed and legally binding, was the deed to the Belleview theatre, naming Troy as the owner.

His hands shaking, tears sliding unnoticed down the slope of his cheeks, Troy rose unsteadily to his feet, unable to think anything for a moment except that once again, when he had found himself losing hope and heart and direction, Matteo had found him. Acknowledging with joy that this was a truth he could cling to, he also acknowledged solemnly that with this—Matteo's parting gift—he could allow himself to once again begin living.

Turning suddenly, half of the papers scattering onto the carpet, he flew toward the bedroom door, intent on retrieving his phone from the coffee table and calling Kasey and Lorelei. Instead he slid to a stop in the living room, eyes wide as Reid Monteforte turned from the doorway, raised a sleek silver revolver, and pointed it at his forehead.

"That idiot with the bulldozer was right about one thing," she said in disgust. "If you want something done, you always have to do it yourself."

She paused, glancing around the condo to determine there were no witnesses before cutting her gaze back to Troy. "You make it too easy, you know," she said, moving closer and smiling cruelly. "You didn't even lock your door." She rolled her eyes. "So here I am, holding all the cards, and there you are, no weapon, no common sense and no one to save you."

Gesturing with the pistol, she backed Troy up against the sofa. "I was sloppy, I admit," she said dryly, her expression disgusted. "I left loose ends, I forged papers myself instead of paying someone else to do it, I didn't think ahead, I didn't cover my tracks." She shook her head sharply. "And I would have walked away from it, cut my losses, abandoned the whole fiasco, but suddenly that damned theatre was in the news, high profile, artists and preservationists making noise, people asking questions, reporters taking pictures of some crazy caterer chaining himself to the fucking doors." She narrowed her eyes. "Who does that?" She shook her head sharply. "Well I'm putting a stop to it. I have too much at stake—this has gone on too long already, and you were too damn close to figuring out the whole thing. You and those girls. Well I'm not going to prison. Did you honestly think I'd let myself be taken down by a caterer and two silly little mermaids?" She took a step closer. "Well think again."

Clutching Matteo's letter and the deed to the theatre as though it could protect him, Troy raised his hands in hopeless defense, as Reid drew the hammer of the pistol back with relish and carefully adjusted her aim.

Chapter Forty One

In Undersea Cottage, as the afternoon sun streamed in through stained glass windows and colored their emotions green and gold and blue, Kasey and Lorelei curled together on the sofa, talking sadly about Troy and angrily about Reid Monteforte. Wrapped in melancholy, in the hush and the colors of the moment, they mourned the futility of fighting for the theatre, even as they acknowledged and appreciated the permanence of their friendship with Troy. Kasey's anger poured out with her tears, and Lorelei held her tenderly close, reaching out to catch each silver drop in the palm of her hand as if she could save them so Kasey would never again have to shed another.

"What kind of person crushes another person's soul, steals their memories, breaks their heart, for nothing more than *money*?" Kasey asked plaintively, her head resting wearily against Lorelei's collarbone, their fingers and hearts entwined. She raised her head, sleek strands of long, dark hair framing her sorrowful face.

Releasing a long, pent up breath, Lorelei shook her head sadly, wishing she had an answer, wishing she could protect Kasey from the chasm that yawned between what was and what should have been, between truth and lies, greed and glory, good people and evil.

"The kind of person who doesn't have a heart," she said softly, brushing Kasey's hair away from her still damp eyes. "I mean, business is business, right? People buy and sell things every day. Products, services, property…"

"Dreams," Kasey said stubbornly, her fingers tightening around Lorelei's hand. "Love, memories, hope and remembrance…it isn't the same."

Lorelei nodded. "That's what I mean," she said, drawing Kasey closer and holding her against her heart, wishing she could protect her forever from ugly truths and lies and deception, and people who didn't care who they hurt. "You're right. It isn't the same at all." She sighed, stretching her feet across the sofa cushions to entwine her legs with Kasey's. "I mean, even from a business perspective, tearing down that theatre should at least make that woman pause, to recognize that she is destroying a great work of art, force her to at least acknowledge the pain it will cause to the person it means the most to. Even if she's still going to do it, she should at least realize the magnitude of what she's destroying…" She shrugged helplessly. "That woman not only doesn't care," she said harshly, her voice thick and low with contempt, "I think she actually revels in it."

Drawing a deep breath that shuddered through her body, Kasey gave in to the last few hiccups of her crying, safe and secure in the arms of this woman who seemed to want nothing more than to hold her forever.

She wanted to rally, to fight, to stand and defend Troy, defend Matteo, defend the doomed and soon to be destroyed theatre—but she had no idea how. Sadly, Lorelei watched the play of emotions across her expressive face and sighed deeply. She had no idea either.

The jangle of Kasey's cell phone sounded suddenly between them, shattering the moment into sharp shards that felt as if they could have drawn blood. Both of them felt utterly raw. Troy's heartache had now become their own, their inability to help him was a secondary wound, and both women felt the pain of being helpless to do anything but love their friend and watch his heart bleed out onto the pavement in front of the Belleview theatre.

Slowly, Kasey drew her phone out of her pocket, staring in great consternation at the screen until Lorelei nudged her.

"What is it, what's wrong?" she asked worriedly, as a faint beep sounded to signal that the person identified on the caller ID had left a message. Her hands unsteady, Kasey swiped the screen icon for voice mail, holding her breath as Cassandra's recorded voice, rushed and shaken, rose from the tiny cell phone speaker.

"Kasey, you were right. You were right and I didn't listen to you. I think Troy is in real danger. Reid said she was going to deal with him permanently, and I'm afraid to even wonder what she means by that. This whole mess with the theatre implicates her in criminal activity, and she'll do whatever it takes to keep that hidden. I understand why Troy wants to save the theatre, but you have to tell him it just isn't worth the risk. I…I'm sorry I didn't listen to you. I'm sorry for that and—well, for everything else." Her voice lowered, became fervent, real emotion filling the words of her warning. "Be careful, Kasey, and tell Troy to be careful too—I think Reid is capable of anything."

Horrified, Kasey looked helplessly at Lorelei, frozen for a moment before leaping from the sofa and seizing the first weapon that came to hand. Her choice, a large blown glass statue of a Siamese fighting fish, was heavy and unwieldy, but in that moment she found herself overtaken with a burning desire to bludgeon Reid Monteforte over the head with an original art piece by Matteo Fabiano. There was a poetic justice to it, and despite her sweet and loving nature, she was currently leaning in favor of blunt force trauma.

Relieving her of the statue, Lorelei handed her the steel baseball bat she kept in the umbrella stand in case of intruders, snatching her car keys from the coffee table and throwing wide the front door. Troy was undoubtedly in imminent danger, and the cavalry was coming.

Chapter Forty Two

Taking scandalous advantage of the lack of traffic police patrolling the streets of downtown Bloomington on a Sunday, Kasey and Lorelei broke speed limits and parked recklessly, thundering across the parking garage and into the elevator only to stand in an agony of impatience as it travelled smoothly upward, unaware of the crisis it precipitated.

When the sleek wood paneled doors opened at last, revealing an empty stretch of tastefully carpeted hallway, the first thing they saw was Troy's door at the end of the passage, unattended and open. Lorelei swore softly.

Reaching into the bag hanging from her shoulder—a breezy, beachy canvas affair in green and white and blue—Lorelei pulled out a compact little pistol. Kasey gasped.

"You know how to shoot a gun?" she whispered in shock.

Lorelei nodded, whispering back. "I played a cop once in a TV commercial."

With that and nothing else on her weapons training resume, she smoothly raised the gun in front of her determined features and moved resolutely down the hallway. After a breathless moment, Kasey followed.

Inside Troy's condo, the culmination of a long gloating speech was rising in the air of late afternoon, the lowering sun casting light through the window to glance off the barrel of Reid Monteforte's revolver. Mocking, contemptuous, she was reveling in Troy's very real fear for his life, taking advantage of his temporary silence to lash at him with cruel words, ensuring that when he went to his death it would be with his heart in ribbons and a bullet in his head.

Troy—fairly certain that his ticket was about to be punched in any case—was considering rushing her in a suicidal campaign if for no other purpose than to bleed maliciously all over her fabulous Gucci open toe heels as he lay dying. It was a poor and petty revenge, but he would take it, by God.

"Don't try it," Reid said silkily, reading his transparent expression and forestalling his fatal heroics. "It's pathetic enough that you are going to die over a building, don't add stupidity to the recipe." She shook her perfectly styled head coldly, every strand of hair forced into obedience and cemented in place. "Is it worth it?" she asked curiously, the pistol still pointed at Troy's forehead. "Dying for a bunch of statues and paintings and gilded hallways created by an artist who died years ago?"

Troy's eyes narrowed as he contemplated whether he could sprint quickly enough across the carpet to die all over her red silk dress as well as her shoes. "You," he said quietly, his muscles tensing for the dash, "are not worthy to even say his name."

Reid laughed, a sound devoid of humor, and high on ridicule. "I admit I made mess of things," she said, indulging in an evil villain speech to go with the designer clutch purse she carried. "Forging the signatures myself was stupid, and I forgot to erase the data entry logs when I erased the records of the sale, but all in all it wasn't a total loss." Her gaze pinned Troy to the carpet like a well-dressed, squirming insect. "I mean, after all, here I am and here you are, and there is only one way this is going to end for both of us." She smiled again, a viper's smile, and gestured with the pistol.

Troy took an inadvisable step toward her, and Reid leveled the gun at his kneecaps. "More gunshots, more blood on the carpet," she said airily, not at all hesitant to inflict crippling wounds in pursuit of her fifteen minutes of gloating. "Though it would be a shame to deface last season's Versace." She glanced admiringly at Troy's suit, one eyebrow grudgingly approving.

Outraged, Troy forgot for a moment that she was holding him at gunpoint. "This suit is *not* last season, you overpriced bitch!" he protested hotly. "It's straight off this season's runway."

Reid smirked, tired of baiting him and ready to finish what she had come there to do. "He made it too easy, you know, just like you did," she said, again taking aim at his forehead.

Troy's expression froze, his heart seeming to stutter in his chest. "Who did?"

"Your former boyfriend," Reid said, lining up the muzzle of the pistol between his fastidiously groomed eyebrows. "He needed a lawyer to handle the escrow accounts and the purchase procedures and, of course, the codicil to the will. Unfortunately for him, he chose my law firm to do it." She shrugged. "Artists," she said heartlessly, unconcerned at admitting the breadth of her perfidy. After all, Troy would soon be dead. Idly, she toyed with the idea of framing that blue haired mermaid girl for his murder.

"I was going to simply take over the property as soon as I heard he was dead, but without the records I had destroyed and the purchase funds I had stolen, it reverted to the former owners and I had to wait for two years while the city chased its tail in circles before deciding to sell," she said, more than willing to air her grievances. "By then it wasn't about the property anymore, it was about not getting caught. Then suddenly I found myself dealing with amateur detectives and inconvenient questions and hysterical former lovers." Her expression hardened. "Well that ends here and now."

An unexpected sound echoed suddenly in the silence, and she turned toward the still open doorway to find Lorelei Desciance, looking disconcertingly competent, pointing a gun in her direction. Behind Lorelei, Kasey Martin stood with a baseball bat in her hands, wearing an expression that dared Reid to ask her why her older brothers had always called her 'Slugger'.

In the moment it took for Reid to register that she was being overthrown by two mermaids and a caterer, Troy had spun on the heel of one Italian leather wingtip and clobbered her with a plaster bust of Jean Paul Gaultier quickly seized from a glass and brass art deco etagere. Stunned, she dropped the gun and fell to the carpet.

"Yeah, yeah, we know," he sneered at her finally silent body. "And you would have gotten away with it too, if it wasn't for us meddling kids."

"Troy!" Kasey cried, dropping the bat and rushing to embrace him. Lorelei kept the gun trained on Reid, in case she showed any signs of stirring.

"Don't worry darling," Troy said brightly, refusing to acknowledge the sheen of sweat that fear had painted on his forehead. "I didn't actually kill her. Even *I* wouldn't look good in prison orange."

Chapter Forty Three

The key that Troy had found in the envelope bearing Matteo's last message of love and devotion fit the lock that graced a wide wooden door set into the wall at the top of a new and ornate staircase in the theatre. Originally a steep and narrow set of steps leading to huge second story scenery vaults and storage areas, the stairs had been replaced with a curving masterpiece of wrought iron, graceful and strong, rising to the second floor like a poem carved of metal and wonder.

Turning the key in the decorative faceplate housing the locking mechanism, Troy looked over his shoulder at Kasey and Lorelei, who stood behind him with hands clasped, breathless with anticipation and caught up in mystery. Turning back to the door, Troy reached for the etched brass doorknob, taking a deep breath before withdrawing the key and gently opening the door. Pausing just inside the threshold of the room beyond, he stood for an indescribable moment, silent and stunned, as if the love he had lost awaited him in these secret rooms above the theatre. In a way, he did.

Once a set of soaring, vast rooms used to house massive set pieces and painted scenery, the rooms above the Belleview theatre had been lovingly transformed, through mastery and art, renovation and magic, clearly fueled by love. Stretching in beautiful lines from the open doorway and across the entire length of the upper story, a home had been painstakingly crafted by the very hands that Troy longed to hold just one more time. Elegant furniture, glorious paintings, graceful statuary and thick carpets filled rooms that bore the unmistakable stamp of Matteo Fabiano's genius and his love.

On a huge carved mahogany table, surrounded by wood chairs with velvet upholstery, a crystal vase of roses stood in mute testament, long dead now and ready to crumble to dust at a touch, but still perfectly formed, exactly as they had been when Matteo had placed them there more than two years earlier. The apartment—a word that scarcely described the opulence and sheer size of the place—had been built as a gift of the heart, but Matteo had died before he could tell anyone that the beautiful home he had hoped to share with Troy existed above the theatre. The letter explaining everything was propped against the crystal vase that held the roses, along with a personal, more private message that brought Troy to tears with its poignancy and promises.

Dried and fragrant, the roses filled the room with a faint spicy scent, memories and heartache blending with loss and remembrance and a love that had never died. On an antique sideboard gracefully carved with intricate patterns, a photograph of Troy and Matteo stood in a heavy silver frame. At its feet, a velvet box bearing two wedding rings rested, their mute question rising in the silence, unasked but not unanswered. For the first time in two long, lonely years, Troy could feel Matteo's arms around him.

Chapter Forty Four

Over the following weeks, as Troy moved his clothes and possessions into the beautiful home Matteo had built for him, his insistence that Kasey move into his old condo bordered on harassment.

"Darling," he persisted, directing burly moving men with patio furniture in the direction of a glassed in solarium on the roof of the theatre, "we simply *must* get you out of that dreadful hole in the wall you call an apartment!" He pointed another set of movers toward the gourmet kitchen by waving a perfectly mixed Mimosa; it was his third that morning. On his hand, the wedding ring Matteo had bought him gleamed faintly, capturing the glow from stained glass light fixtures hanging gracefully from the ceiling. The other ring, which would have been Matteo's, he wore on a gold chain around his neck.

Stepping in to prevent him from a full scale sales pitch, Lorelei laid a hand on his impeccable sleeve and fixed her eyes on Kasey.

"She doesn't need a place to live, Troy," she said, reaching out to take Kasey's hand in hers. "She has a place to live—with me, at Undersea Cottage." She turned to slip her arms around Kasey, leaving no doubt that she meant the offer with every beat of her heart. "That is, if she wants to."

Taken aback, Kasey returned the embrace, a rush of joy flooding through her as Lorelei's smile lit up the room and echoed her own. "Yes," she said quietly, leaning forward to kiss the lips that parted just in time to meet her. "Oh yes."

As the kiss deepened, lingered, filling up with heat and promise, Troy grinned in satisfaction and went to fix himself another Mimosa.

"After all, darlings," he said to no one—fully prepared to take every bit of credit for bringing them together— "*somebody* has to congratulate me!"

The grand opening of the Matteo Fabiano Memorial Theatre found Troy flitting happily around the gilded halls of the magnificent renovation, wearing a tuxedo that cost as much as his vintage sports car and tippling sparkling champagne. Fiendishly pleased, he took a moment to remember that Reid Monteforte was probably experiencing a dearth of champagne at the Indiana women's prison in Indianapolis. Thanks to the eye witness accounts of Lorelei and Kasey, his own deposition, and the enthusiastically shared evidence provided to the court by Allison Inglis, it was likely to be a very long time before Reid saw another glass of champagne. As was only right.

Greeting and mingling with a bevy of elegant guests, Troy finally paused in the red velvet carpeted hallway that led to the dressing rooms, where Kasey and Lorelei stood before tall, ornate mirrors, wearing fairy tale wedding dresses, glittering necklaces and jeweled mermaid crowns.

Their suggestion that the wedding be a small, private affair at Undersea Cottage had scandalized him for days, and he had timed their ceremony to coincide with the opening of both the glorious theatre and Jorge's newly opened patisserie adjacent to the first floor salon. He had not spent ten months preparing the theatre to reopen for nothing, he pointed out, and the tuxedo he wore was a custom tailored Armani that he needed an excuse to show off. Did they really want to rob him of his moment? As usual, his theatrics had the desired effect, and Kasey and Lorelei agreed to hold the wedding at the theatre. Making him their maid of honor was just icing on the cake (which was created in sumptuous perfection by Jorge) and Troy wasted no time digging out the four leftover champagne fountains he still had gathering dust in a storage unit.

So in the end, Lorelei and Kasey lived in a mermaid cottage under the sea. Even though they didn't, really. It was complicated, but at the same time perfectly simple. They lived in a house called Undersea Cottage because they met, fell in love, and got married, and their best friend Troy turned their wedding into the unqualified social event of the century. No seafood was served at the reception.

Dedicated with anonymous gratitude
and sincere admiration to the inimitable M.
(who lives for glitter, not you).
His creative vision, defiance of convention,
determination in the face of obstacles,
and unapologetic originality has reignited mine.

About the Author

Tallulah Burns is an independent author who spends her days in Florida, writing novels, singing torch songs, buying vintage accessories and catering to the whims of a spoiled dog who is the biggest little diva this side of Miami. When not plotting books while wearing glamorous sunglasses, Tallulah travels in search of story ideas and eclectic shopping opportunities. *Last Minute Mermaid* is the third in her collection of romances featuring lesbian characters, happily ever afters, and heroines with heart. Check out her first two best-selling titles, **Safe Haven** and **Celia Moon, Seventh Wonder**, both available through Amazon.com, Kindle and Kindle Unlimited.

Author's Note

The town of Bloomington Indiana is a wonderful, colorful place, filled with diversity, art, music and the seeking of knowledge. A college town surrounding the University of Indiana, it thrums with a quintessential creative energy, its shops and landmarks, coffee houses included, welcoming students and artists and tourists with equal hospitality. The coffee shop in this book (*Karma Sumatra*) is loosely based on SOMA coffee, a coffee house on Kirkwood avenue in the heart of Bloomington, where I wrote the first drafts of both *Safe Haven* and *Celia Moon, Seventh Wonder*, after flying from Florida to visit friends in Bloomington. As my friends both had full time jobs, I was dropped off (by request) at the coffee house every morning during the work week and stayed at "coffee day care" until they picked me up after work in the evening. I love spending time at coffee day care in Bloomington! The description of the deliciously eccentric coffee house is not at all exaggerated, and is only embellished in occasional particulars, and if you ever visit SOMA coffee in Bloomington Indiana, you will find yourself surrounded by the quirkiest, most colorful environment you could hope for (though I can't promise free pity pastries.) I have written thousands upon thousands of words at SOMA and hope to return soon to write thousands upon thousands of words more. Florence Henderson (not the actress) is – quite unfortunately – completely fabricated, as is Jorge the pastry god.

Matteo Fabiano's gorgeous theatre was inspired in part by the Tampa Theatre in Tampa Florida, the exquisite creation of architect John Eberson in 1926. It too was slated for demolition but was saved and named to the National Register of Historic Places in 1978 and designated as a landmark of the city of Tampa in 1988. This designation thus protects it from destruction even without the assistance of a gorgeous gay caterer nobly chaining himself to the entrance doors in a dramatic and romantic gesture while wearing designer clothing. In my opinion, the Tampa theatre—home to both stage and silver screen—is the best possible place to watch the original version of Casablanca, preferably whilst sipping champagne and wearing 1940's period clothing. Of all the theatres in all the towns in all the world, believe me, you should walk into that one.

XOXOXO

Love, Tallulah

Safe Haven
by Tallulah Burns

Jasmine Delacourt has just left a two-year relationship after her girlfriend cheated on her. She is determined to live a solitary life and never trust another woman with her heart again. Looking for a new beginning, she purchases a vintage house in New York. Charming but dilapidated, the house requires the frequent services of a renovation and repair company. The owner of the company—whose unhealthy habits have led to orders from his doctor—grudgingly turns over the business to Shaughnessy Callahan, his niece-by-marriage, a gorgeous redhead who is handy with a hammer, currently unattached, and determined to stay that way. Within days of meeting Shaughnessy, Jasmine receives a vague and threatening note, and is approached by a man in town who asks bewildering questions. Two days later the man turns up dead. While news of the murder shakes the town, Jasmine tries to bury her fears (and her growing attraction to Shaughnessy) in work. Frightening clues in Jasmine's house point to a past that is tied to the murder, and Shaughnessy and Jasmine work to solve the mystery before anyone else— including them—can be hurt or killed because of it. Whatever past secrets the old house is hiding, the intrigue and danger surrounding them are still very much alive. Avoiding danger, collecting clues and solving a murder is not exactly the perfect setting for two women intent on avoiding complications to find romance with one another. Then again, maybe it is.

Celia Moon, Seventh Wonder
By Tallulah Burns

As far as the town of Serendipity was concerned, six of the seven wonders of the world resided in the state of Georgia. As far as Celia Moon was concerned, she qualified as the seventh. A fierce and creative individual, she is used to raising eyebrows, and has always fought a rebellious battle against fulfilling the expectations of others. Serendipity—a tiny town of old-school conformists—breathed a collective sigh of relief the day that Celia donned a Picasso emblazoned T-shirt, a black lace skirt and teal velvet combat boots, packed up her art supplies, guitar and a half-written novel, mounted a second-hand motorcycle and disappeared down the interstate. Now Celia has returned to Serendipity, as wild and independent as she ever was, fighting hard to be herself in a place that still wants her to be like everybody else. Fresh from a whirlwind of international travel, Del Carrington is a successful designer who has come to Serendipity to care for her elderly grandfather. Turning her back on a life of high fashion and glamour, she soon discovers that in all her travels, she has never met anyone quite like Celia Moon. Leaving behind a past she wants to forget, Del comes to Serendipity driven by heartbreak and a painful secret. As time passes, she discovers that Celia has done the same. Can their hearts learn to trust one other enough to take a chance on love, and share the secrets that keep them apart? If they can, it will be a wonder.

Printed in Great Britain
by Amazon